Odd Lot

Stories to Chill the Heart

STEVE BURT

**Illustrations by
Jessica Hagerman**

**Burt
Creations**

Norwich, CT

Odd Lot
Stories to Chill the Heart

Copyright © 2001 by
Steven E. Burt

First Printing, 2001
Second Printing, 2002
Third Printing, 2003
Fourth Printing, 2005

ISBN 10   0-9649283-2-9
ISBN 13   978-0-9649283-2-9

Printed in USA

Inquiries should be addressed to:

Burt
Creations

Steve Burt
29 Arnold Place
Norwich, CT 06360

T 866-693-6936
F 860-889-4068
www.burtcreations.com

Illustrations by Jessica Hagerman
Design by Dotti Albertine

Screaming Readers

Steve Burt's work keeps you guessing with a savvy blend of unusual characters and unexpected situations. Just when you think you have the story cornered, you'll find it's sneaked up and gripped you by the back of the neck instead.

— BILL HUGHES, EDITOR, *DREAD* MAGAZINE

Steven E. Burt's new book, Odd Lot, *is sure to be a winner and a good read. With chilling stuff like "The Mason's Leech" and good, offbeat speculative fiction like "Casino Night," how could it not be? At* Black Petals *we're always glad to see Mr. Burt's byline.*

— KENNETH JAMES CRIST, EDITOR, *BLACK PETALS*
HORROR/SCIENCE FICTION MAGAZINE

If ever there was an author to rival the storytelling genius of M.R. James and E.F. Benson, Steve Burt is it. Eerie and compelling, Burt's prose will have you relishing those lonely places where light dare not tread.

— DON H. LAIRD, PUBLISHER, *CROSSOVER PRESS,*
THRESHOLD MAGAZINE

Steve Burt has a firm grasp of the unsettling and the uncanny . . . His stories are set in a recognisable world, but they never go in the obvious direction, preferring instead to take off down dark alleys and twisting roads which leave the reader shivering and looking nervously into dark corners when the book is closed.

— BARBARA RODEN, EDITOR, *ALL HALLOWS*
(THE MAGAZINE OF THE GHOST STORY SOCIETY)

Other Sightings

"Lighthouse Moths" was published simultaneously in *Lincoln County Weekly* (Maine), October 28, 1999 and *The Threshold,* Winter 1999-2000, and was named HONORABLE MENTION in *The Year's Best Fantasy & Horror #13*, July 2000.

"Garden Plot" was published simultaneously in *Beyond the Moon*, Winter 1994-1995 (Second Prize, Horror) and in *All Hallows #8* (The Ghost Story Society, England), February 1995, and was named HONORABLE MENTION In *The Year's Best Fantasy & Horror #9*, July 1996.

"The Mason's Leech" was published in *Beyond the Moon*, Fall 1994 (First Prize, Horror), later in the acclaimed anthology, *Midnight Never Comes* (British Columbia, Canada: Ash-Tree Press, 1997), and was named HONORABLE MENTION in *The Year's Best Fantasy & Horror #11*, July 1998.

"The Strand" was published in Dread, Spring 2000, and was named an HONORABLE MENTION in *The Year's Best Fantasy & Horror #14,* July 2001.

"Casino Night" was published in *Psychotrope* (England), Spring 2000, and was named an HONORABLE MENTION in the *The Year's Best Fantasy & Horror #14,* July 2001.

"The Witness Tree" was published in the acclaimed anthology, *Shadows and Silence* (British Columbia: Ash-Tree Press, 2000). It was named HONORABLE MENTION in *The Year's Best Fantasy & Horror* #14, July 2001.

"Captain James's Bones" was published in *All Hallows #25* (The Ghost Story Society, Canada), October 2000.

"The Ice Fisherman" was published in a newspaper, *The Peconic Bay Shopper,* September 1994, then in a number of literary magazines including *Belletrist Review, Potomac Review, Reader's Break,* and *Potpourri.*

"Where Lions Hide" is new.

Thanks to

. . . Jessica Hagerman for the great illustrations.

. . . the following people in an amazing sequence of events: Rev. Fred Franzius who, as a special treat around Halloween, read one of my first spooky (and unsubmitted anywhere) stories aloud to his congregation at Mohegan Congregational Church in Uncasville, Connecticut, where Dick Fawcett, an aficionado of the classic English ghost story, heard it and sent it (along with two other of my stories) to Rosemary Pardoe, editor of Ghosts and Scholars, in England, who passed it on to Barbara and Christopher Roden at The Ghost Story Society where, as co-editors of the Society's All Hallows magazine, they published "Garden Plot" and "Uncle Bando's Chimes," then, as co-publishers at the World Fantasy-Award-winning and Bram Stoker-Award-winning Ash-Tree Press, they published "The Mason's Leech" in their prestigious hardcover anthology, Midnight Never Comes. So the first three supernatural tales were stories I never even submitted on my own. And all three gained me Honorable Mentions in Year's Best Fantasy & Horror. Thanks, Fred, Dick, Rosemary, Barbara and Christopher.

. . . all the small press editors who printed my stories and built my confidence.

. . . Dotti Albertine at Albertine Book Design, Santa Monica, who designed the front and back covers and the book's interior. Dotti is already at work on several other books I've got coming out.

. . . Nancy Kram at Kram Communications in Los Angeles.

. . . Dan Poynter, the guru of self-publishing, who taught me so much and put me in touch with the right people at the right time.

. . . Ellen Reid, who has been the ramrod (organizer/team coordinator/you name it) for several of my projects now. She, more than anyone, saw my potential as a popular author.

About the Cover Artist

JESSICA E. HAGERMAN is a freelance illustrator from Southold, Long Island. She works primarily in pen and ink. Jessica currently resides in Massachusetts with her cat, Simon, and is using her degree in Art Therapy from Springfield College by working with the children at Shriners' Hospital in Springfield. She recently went back to school to work on her Masters degree in Art Therapy. *Odd Lot* is the first book Jessie has illustrated and she hopes it's not her last.

About the Author

STEVE BURT'S life reads like one of his stories; it's a good life, a genuine life, with plenty of plot to make it interesting.

Since 1979 Steve has been a pastor, church consultant, seminary professor, church executive, and very popular keynote speaker, mixing humor and stories in with his teaching.

Graduating high school complete with academic and sports honors and having edited the school newspaper, Steve went into the Navy for a four-year hitch. He wrote for the ship newsletter, continued to excel at sports, and in 1969 married his high school sweetheart, Jo Ann. The next year their daughter, Wendy, was born.

In 1983 Steve received a Master's Degree from Bangor Theological Seminary. In 1987 he completed a four-year doctorate program in three years and graduated at the top of his class at Andover Newton Theological School.

In 2004, just as *Wicked Odd*, the fourth in the Stories to Chill the Heart Series, was hitting bookshelves, Steve's third, *Oddest Yet*, won horror's top prize, the Bram Stoker award for Young Adults. His *Even Odder* was a runnerup to Harry Potter for the 2003 Stoker. He earned three Ray Bradbury awards in 2003 and 2004.

In addition to chilling stories, like those in *Odd Lot*, Steve also writes stories that warm the heart, *A Christmas Dozen*, and touch the heart, *Unk's Fiddle*.

Not what you might expect from your average Reverend Doctor / Pastor / Author. But somehow it's right on target for Steve Burt. What's next? Stay tuned.

Also by Steve Burt

Wicked Odd
Still More Stories to Chill the Heart
Burt Creations 2005

Oddest Yet
Even More Stories to Chill the Heart
Burt Creations 2004

Even Odder
More Stories to Chill the Heart
Burt Creations 2003

A Christmas Dozen
Christmas Stories to Warm the Heart
Burt Creations 2000 (paperback)
2001 (audiobook) 2002 (hardcover)

The Little Church That Could
Raising Small Church Esteem
Judson Press 2000

Unk's Fiddle
Stories to Touch the Heart
Steven E. Burt 1995 (hardcover)
Burt Creations 2001 (paperback)

What Do You Say to a Burning Bush?
Sermons for the Season After Pentecost
CSS Publishing 1995

My Lord, He's Loose in the World!
Meditations on the Meaning of Easter
Brentwood Christian Press 1994

Raising Small Church Esteem
with Hazel Roper
Alban Institute 1992

Christmas Special Delivery
Stories and Meditations for Christmas
Fairway Press 1991

Fingerprints on the Chalice
Contemporary Communion Meditations
CSS Publishing 1990

Activating Leadership in the Small Church
Clergy and Laity Working Together
Judson Press 1988

Introduction

Radio and newspaper interviewers always ask me, "Why ghost and horror stories?"

Well, it's like this. My siblings, friends, and I grew up in scary times, the fifties and sixties. We learned in school how to hide under our desks in case an atom bomb was dropped. (I still remember my father's Civil Defense helmet on top of the refrigerator, to be donned in case he had to become one of the traffic coordinators if we were attacked.) We were to be on guard at all times against spies and infiltrators. We heard of laser beam weapons and a neutron bomb that could destroy people without harming property.

We dealt with those fears in vicarious ways. We found safe entertainments that chilled our spines, fired our imaginations, and allowed us to vent our fears--books, comic books, movies, campfire tales. Afterward, things returned to normal and we discovered we were safe again.

Every month we awaited the arrival of the newest issue of such comics as *Weird Tales, Tales of the Unexpected,* or *Tales from the Crypt.* Even the GI comics had a supernatural version, *The Haunted Tank* (one of my favorites). TV was fairly new, but our parents let us watch Rod Serling's *Twilight Zone, Alfred Hitchcock Theater*, and *The Outer Limits,* all of which we talked eagerly about with friends at school and playground. We loved being scared, we loved delving into the bizarre and supernatural—so long as it was an entertainment and we were safe afterward. So I always loved it, just the way kids today grab up fresh stories in R.L.Stine's *Goosebumps* series. It's good fun, and it's safe.

But besides being entertaining, stories of the bizarre and supernatural raised issues, warned us. Didn't George Orwell warn us that "Big Brother Is Watching?" In *Kubrick's 2001: A Space Odyssey,* remember Hal the computer (artificial intelligence) rebelling against his creators? Or how about *Frankenstein?* Even Charles Dickens' ghost story, *A Christmas Carol,* is a warning about

Scroogism (don't let your penurious heart shivel up!). Look at Hitchcock's movie, *The Birds* (environmental rebellion). There are dangers associated with space travel, with atomic energy, cloning, biological research, all sorts of things. Writers of bizarre and supernatural fiction may not be the first ones to call attention to an issue, danger, or hazard, but they're often the first to embody the danger or issue so it can be examined. Many people need to feel about something before they think about and act on it.

So some of my stories are pure entertainment, campfire tales to chill the spine. But in some I seek to educate or warn, too. "Captain James's Bones" is purely a campfire entertainment tale with a mild warning about the dangers of practical jokes. "Garden Plot" is also a campfire tale that points out the dangers of belittling another's beliefs while self-righteously taking the supposed higher ground. "Casino Night" is my response to the dangers of gambling. "Where Lions Hide" is an environmental concern. The other stories, too, are blends of entertainment (a good scare) and warnings (something to make us feel, then think).

Welcome to Weird Theater. Check your popcorn closely before you eat it. (Bet you can't tell if it's genetically engineered corn.) Enjoy the show.

CONTENTS

Lighthouse Moths

"Lighthouse Moths" is more than a ghost story; it's a story about the power of love and redemption. Ellen Datlow, horror editor of the prestigious *Year's Best Fantasy and Horror*, called it "lovely and moving" and named it an Honorable Mention in *YBF&H #13*. The story appeared in *Lincoln County Weekly* (Damariscotta, ME), October 28, 1999; *Threshold Magazine*, Winter 1999-2000; *Peconic Bay Shopper* (Southold, NY), February 2000; *Tales of the Unanticipated* (Minnesota Science Fiction Society), April 2000.

I was sitting at the front desk daydreaming when the screen door clapped shut and a very tall man stepped into the lobby area. I didn't recognize him at first. He was gaunt and looked exhausted—a bone-weary, sleepless-nights, haunted sort of exhaustion. He reminded me of a fifty-pounds-lighter version of someone from the past whom my mind couldn't quite draw a bead on. But my gut told me the man I was trying to recall was more affable and outgoing. This man by the door was a shadow of somebody I once knew.

"Hello, Mr. Duncan," said a vaguely familiar voice, but one without much timbre or resonance. This man's voice sounded timid, beaten down, lacking any real—*energy*? No. *Life*. This voice lacked life. He crossed the room and set his suitcase on the floor beside him.

"How've you been, Dunc?" he said, shifting to the nickname everyone used. He straightened closer to his full height, about six-five. That's when I recognized him.

"Roger," I said, thrusting my hand toward his as I slid from my stool. "Roger Angleford. I'll be damned. I wasn't expecting you."

That's what I said: *I wasn't expecting you.* But I thought: *Roger Angleford, you poor sad tormented S.O.B., I never expected to see you again—not ever. Not after your daughter's death here three years ago.*

Angleford smiled a weak, mouth-only smile, no sparkle to his eyes. Beneath his dark-circled eyes hung puffy bags of skin, the result of a weight drop, I figured, whose underlying cause must have been unrelenting grief.

"You look good, Roger," I lied. "Dropped a few extra pounds."

Angleford ignored my idiotic pleasantry and I felt stupid for even uttering it.

"So, what brings you to Pemaquid?" I asked, making sure not to say *back* to Pemaquid. I needed to proceed with caution; God only knew, this poor man's nights—days, too, no doubt—had been Hell on Earth, filled with pain, soul pain, after the tragic loss of his only child. He had returned not just to Maine, but to Pemaquid Point where, on a windy afternoon in late August, the day after a hurricane grazed Cape Cod and pounding surf drew sightseers to the shore all along the Maine coast, a huge wave—a killer wave, the papers had dubbed it—had swept his beloved eleven year-old daughter from the rocky peninsula below the lighthouse.

He gazed past me at a painting of Pemaquid Light on the wall behind me and said dreamily, "Couldn't help myself. Something ... *drew* me."

While Roger Angleford stood transfixed by the painting, my own mind called up a snapshot I had taken of the Anglefords their next-to-last summer at Pemaquid Inn. They mugged for me on the porch while I used their camera to take a family photo. There

stood tall, muscular Roger making a goofy face under his off-kilter golf cap, thick hands clapped around the shoulders of the two women he loved: his petite Asian wife Suki grinning and sticking her tongue out through the strings of her tennis racket, and their sometimes precocious, always curious daughter Cara looking into the camera through a pair of binoculars, her frizzy flame-red hair poofing out from under a tan straw sun hat. Oh, that red hair—one couldn't forget that burning red hair. Later they mailed an extra print to me from

Connecticut, with a hand-lettered caption: American (Vacation) Gothic.

"I know it's short notice, Dunc," Angleford said, forcing us both to come back down to Earth. "And I understand how busy the inn is this time of year, but ... any chance you've got an empty room? Say, for three nights?"

I felt like Angleford had just guessed the King of Spades hidden behind my back.

"Roger," I said. "Incredible as this may sound, a couple from Massachusetts had to leave on short notice this morning. A death in the wife's family, so they had to drive back to Massachusetts to make funeral arrangements."

"Wow," he said, but without any real enthusiasm in his voice.

"It frees up a room for three nights," I said, wanting to whistle a few notes from the *Twilight Zone* theme song. But I didn't, because Angleford's reaction was flat.

"I'll take it," he said, handing me his charge card as he reached to fill out the register. "Twenty-eighth, -ninth, thirtieth."

When I heard him say the dates out loud, it struck me that this was the final week of August, his week, their week, the Anglefords'. A question I didn't dare ask formed in my head: *Did Cara die on the thirtieth or the thirty-first?* I couldn't remember, and knowing the answer wasn't essential, but it was one of those things that'd gnaw at me until I found out. I was sure it was one of those two days, though. Was that why he was here, to mark an anniversary date, to mark it with a memorial service of some kind?

"Suki?" I asked, wondering if perhaps she was in the car waiting to hear if we had a vacancy. I knew the answer to my question as soon as I asked it. She wasn't with him. She wouldn't return to Pemaquid. Nor would it have surprised me to learn the Anglefords had divorced or were divorcing, citing as cause a three-year wedge of grief.

"Suki's home," he said. "Coping much better than I am. She's got every door and window in the house open. Screens off, too." Then, noting my puzzlement, he explained.

"Old Chinese custom. At certain times of the year— festival days, anniversaries, you know—they open up the home so their departed ancestors can come visit."

"Cara?" I asked.

"No," he said, his eyes two deep wells of pain.

For a moment I feared Angleford had misunderstood the meaning of my question. Had he misheard and thought I'd forgotten Cara was dead, thought I was asking if she'd be staying the three nights, too? If so, he'd think me worse than forgetful, he'd judge me to be horribly insensitive. But when he continued, I knew he had understood.

"Not yet," he said. "Parents, grandparents, aunts, uncles, Suki says. Not Cara."

Angleford pocketed his room key, picked up his luggage, and nodded a thank-you-and-good-day. He started up the stairs toward his room, trudging like a man mounting a gallows. Was it the past three years or was it this particular pilgrimage back to Pemaquid Point that was draining him so?

I thought about Suki welcoming the dead as houseguests, and how Roger Angleford had reported No Cara as if it were a simple fact, like saying there's no mail today. I tried to imagine a gauzy, lace-like Christmasangel version of Cara Angleford drifting in through a window on the breeze. It was then that I remembered her body had never been recovered from wherever the undertow dragged it. For her funeral they had used her school photo on an empty casket.

I saw Angleford again around suppertime—mine, not his. He passed the dining room on his way out the front door, looking less haggard, perhaps from a nap and shower. He waved and called, "Dinner out. Don't wait up."

I didn't. Roger Angleford was a grown man. Nevertheless I noticed he hadn't returned by ten-thirty when I went to bed.

Next morning I sat in the dining room, sipping my coffee and reading the *Lincoln County Weekly*. The chair opposite mine scraped the floor and I glanced up to see Roger Angleford sliding onto the seat.

"Lighthouse moths," he said, skipping any early morning pleasantries.

"What?" I said, expecting at least a good morning.

"You know," Angleford said, slowly and distinctly enunciating each syllable, giving each the same weight the way an impatient teacher speaks to a child. "Light house moths." His eyes bore into me.

"Geez, Roger," I said. "Lighthouse moths? You've visited here enough years. You know about it. A myth. An old wives' tale. Tourist malarkey."

"Come on, Dunc," he pressed. "There's more."

"What more?" I said. "Are you referring to history—Captain James's schooner smashing on the Pemaquid rocks in a storm with the loss of all hands, including his wife and daughters and crew? Hell, Roger, that's all in the Bristol Town records and a dozen other library books. Every person in this town and most of the tourists know the shipwreck story."

He didn't relax his gaze.

"Look, Roger, " I said. "Who've you been talking to? Jacko? Not Jacko Landon? At the lounge, right? Cripes, Roger, he's the town drunk. He's a clown. A whopper swapper. Loves an audience and anybody who'll buy him a drink. Spreads more manure than a dairy farmer. Oh sure, he's a spellbinder. But the one about the lighthouse moths? Don't you see? Jacko. John O. Landon. Jacko Landon. Get it? Like jack-o-lantern. Campfire tales go with his nickname. Halloween, ghosts, goblins, witches."

I thought I had ended my tirade emphatically, but Angleford kept a steady gaze on me and I could see he wasn't convinced. The man was hurting and desperate, and I felt sorry for him, but I didn't want to help Jacko kindle false hopes in Roger. I hated to see him make a fool of himself. Yet I also saw before me a different man from the day before, a Roger Angleford much more animated.

"Okay, Roger," I said. "Lighthouse moths. Captain James's shipwreck is a fact. Lighthouse moths are fiction, the made-up part, the add-on myth that keeps it interesting. Some say it's huge moths, others say disembodied spirits, lost souls, attracted to the beacon in the lighthouse. Jacko probably told you the most common version—that it's the ghosts of Captain James, his family and crew, right?"

"Actually," Angleford said, "Jacko says it's only three of them—Captain James, his wife, and one of the daughters—the three whose bodies were lost to the sea."

"Oh," I said, beginning to see where this was going. I tried to stay with the germ of the myth rather than go back to Cara's death. "I suppose Jacko mentioned it's only on the full moon? Or did he tell it this time as harvest moon, or blue moon, or wolf moon?" I had never put any stock in ghost stories and refused to take them seriously now.

"Blue moon. The second full moon in the same month," Angleford said in defense of his new-found bar buddy, Jacko. "Swears he's seen them swirling around up there dozens of times."

"That's crap," I said. "When?"

"Like he said, on the second full moon of the month. Dozens of times—maybe more—over the years."

"That's what I've heard, too," I said. "Second full moon. Not that I believe Jacko's seen anything. I was just making sure you had the straight story."

Angleford nodded as if I had just offered an apology.

"Want to hear my theory?" I said, and he nodded again. "I think in the summer there are always moths in the lighthouse, regardless of the moon. But at night when they fly around that thousand-watt bulb, it projects their shadows out through the lens, and it magnifies their shadows. Kind of like a slide projector, as I see it. Simple as that. Moths, yes, but regular size ones. With giant shadows. And no Captain James, no wife, no daughter—no ghosts. That's tourist fodder, helps sell souvenirs."

After a moment he said, "Thanks for the theory, Dunc. Makes sense." He stood and went up to his room.

I carried my breakfast dishes to the kitchen and set them in the sink. As I ran some water over them I glanced at the calendar next to the wall phone. The thirty-first would be a full moon, the second full moon in August. The gnawing came back into my brain then. Which day had Cara drowned, the thirtieth or the thirty-first? If it had been the thirty-first, why hadn't Angleford asked for four nights instead of three? Was he planning some sort of symbolic letting-go service for the last morning, after which he'd drive home to Connecticut?

Suddenly Angleford's head appeared in the doorway to the kitchen.

"Dunc," he said. "I need your help. How can I get into the lighthouse?"

I couldn't help shaking my head in disbelief.

LIGHTHOUSE MOTHS

"You can't," I said. "You know that, Roger. The Coast Guard took it over from the old Lighthouse Service and maintains the tower and beacon. The keeper's house has been turned over to the Town of Bristol, which maintains Pemaquid Point Lighthouse Park. Downstairs is the Fisherman's Museum, which I'm sure you've visited on past vacations, and the upstairs is an apartment that's rented to a nice couple. But it'll take the Coast Guard to get through the tower door, which is inside the back room of the museum. The Coast Guard isn't likely to offer you a guided tour."

"But people get up there," Angleford said.

"Members of the Lighthouse Preservation Society," I said. "Special—"

"You're a member, aren't you?" he interrupted.

"Yes," I said. "But, as I was trying to tell you, the Coast Guard takes them up, and that's once a year on their fall tour. You need reservations, and it's not until October, I think. Not even members of the Preservation Society have keys."

Angleford harrumphed and stood with his arms crossed, then tried another tack.

"What's the name of the people in the apartment?" he asked.

"I really don't recall, Roger," I lied, hoping he'd let it go at that. I didn't want them to think I'd sent Angleford over to pester them.

"Roger," I said, changing the subject. "What day did Cara—" I found I couldn't say die or drown.

"The thirty-first," he said, his words casting a pall over the moment. "Why?"

"Oh," I said, "I was just wondering if you were planning a little private memorial service to mark the date. Because if you were," I said, surprised to hear the words come out of my mouth, "I'd be happy to share in it with you."

"Thanks, Dunc," he said, his mouth tightening as he fought back tears. "Thanks, no."

I wasn't clear if he was saying no to my offer or no, he wasn't planning anything.

***

"Good morning, Dunc. I need a favor."

I looked up from my morning coffee and saw Angleford towering over the table.

"Something to eat, Roger? Coffee?" I motioned to the chair opposite me.

"No, thanks," he said. "I've got to get to town and pick up a few things. Just one item you may be able to help me with, though, if I could borrow it."

"What is it, Roger?" I said.

"A ladder. An extension ladder." Angleford smiled a rubbery Dick Van Dyke grin, a Stan Laurel grin. "Pretty please?"

I stared up at him. "It's not for what I think it's for, is it? You're not planning to scale a local castle wall or parapet, are you?"

"Dunc, I just asked to borrow a ladder. If you wanted to borrow one from me, would I give you the third degree? Yes or no?" he asked, giving me a shaming look.

"It's in the second barn, the yellow Victorian with the colored lobster buoys hanging all over the front of it," I said. "Once you're in the garage door go to the right. There's an aluminum extension ladder hanging from wall pegs. Just put it back when you're done."

"Thanks, Dunc," Angleford said, straightening up from his crouch. "You're a friend."

"Roger," I said. "You may be able to reach the outer catwalk of the lighthouse, but you can't get inside to the inner catwalk. There are huge thick window panels all the way around, and the only way to the inner catwalk is to come up the spiral staircase."

"I know," he said. "I've read up on it and spoken to a couple who know the light. I just want to look."

"Today?" I said.

"Tonight," he answered. "I've got stuff to get in town."

Angleford returned and had supper at the inn that night for the first time. He said nothing about his business in town nor about the evening mission he intended. He went out to the barn before dark, strapped the aluminum extension ladder onto his car roof, and quietly turned out the driveway toward Pemaquid Point Lighthouse. For a moment I thought about phoning his wife, Suki, but decided against it. I half-expected to receive a late-night call from the State Police, saying they had Roger Angleford in custody and could I vouch for him. But the call never came.

I tried to forget about Angleford and slept fitfully, finally getting up at two-thirty. I looked outside and saw that his car wasn't in the parking area. Nor was my extension ladder on its pegs in the barn. But a light shone from the two windows of Angleford's room. Had he walked back to the inn on foot? I climbed to the second floor hallway and knocked lightly on his door.

No one answered. Sound asleep? I doubted it. I put a hand on the knob, twisted it and pushed the door lightly. It swung open.

"Roger?" I whispered. Then louder, "Roger, are you all right?"

The bureau lamp and the two lamps on either bedside table were on. On the bed, bureau, desk, and tables were photos, albums, scrapbooks, Father's Day and birthday cards. Angleford had created a shrine to Cara, his tribute, his way of remembering her. Three teddy bears and two dolls sat with their backs against the headboard of the bed.

I felt worse than an intruder. I was violating someone's sacred ground. But before I could back out, movements caught my eye, shadows where two walls came together with the ceiling near one of the bedside table lamps.

Moths! Moths darting and fluttering around the light bulb, their shadows projecting onto the surfaces around them. I glanced at the other lamps in the room. They all had moths beating themselves against their hot bulbs. Where had they come from?

The windows. The open windows. I crossed the floor and saw that not only were the windows up, but the screens were, too. The moths were flying in from outside, attracted to the lamps in Angleford's shrine to his daughter. I reached to lower the screen, then decided not to. Roger would know I'd violated the sanctity of his room. Instead I backed out, closed the door behind me, and tried to go back to sleep.

At 5:30 a.m., my usual time to get up, I put on a pot of coffee. Shortly after first light Angleford's car pulled into the parking area. He got out, replaced the ladder in the barn, and came inside.

"Ladder's back, Dunc," he said with an honest smile that showed a few teeth. There was a faint sparkle, a sign of life in his eyes that showed even through his exhaustion. I was certain he'd not only been out all night, but up all night.

"Hungry, Roger?" I said, hoping to hear what had happened.

"No, thanks. I'm beat," he said. "Time for a little shut-eye. Checkout still 11 a.m.?"

I nodded, and upstairs to his shrine he went.

At 11 a.m. Angleford was plopping his luggage in front of my registration desk and handing over his room key.

"Dunc," he said. "I can't begin to say how much

I've appreciated your patience with me these couple of days." He added in a choked voice, "And your caring," and clasped my hand between his hands in a warm handshake.

"You're welcome, Roger," I said. "I know it's been hard."

He nodded and backed away, luggage in hand, his lip trembling. I watched him load his suitcase into the back seat of his car and climb in. When he got to the end of the driveway, he didn't turn toward the mainland. He turned toward Pemaquid Point. *A final good-bye before heading home to Connecticut and Suki?* It was none of my business. Roger Angleford had checked out and was on his own. A part of me felt sorry, but I was also relieved to see him go. I didn't think I could stand another day of his pain.

Around five o'clock the phone rang. It was the woman who lived in the apartment above the Fisherman's Museum. She said the man who had knocked on her door two days before to inquire about the lighthouse, the man who had claimed he was a friend of mine and was staying at my inn, had been parked outside her apartment all day, watching her place through binoculars. Her husband was away and, although she assured me she wasn't frightened, she admitted Roger's surveillance made her a bit nervous. She asked if I thought she should call the police. I explained Roger's situation and recapped Cara's death, then promised I'd go and speak with him. I said I could almost guarantee he'd be home in Connecticut the next day, but she thanked me and said she'd just as soon spend the night at her sister's in Newcastle.

I phoned Charlie, my 83 year-old relief clerk, and asked him to cover for me so I could go look for Angleford. My plan was to convince him to join me for dinner at one of the restaurants in Damariscotta.

The sun was about to set when I trotted into the lighthouse parking area searching for Angleford's car. The cars were hard to distinguish in the dusk. A couple near the lighthouse looked similar in shape and color to Angleford's—but they lacked Connecticut plates. I swung my arms and toured the dirt and gravel lot, pretending I was speed walking for exercise. Finally I saw Connecticut license plates on a silver Honda at the lower end of the lot, the view overlooking the rocks Cara had been swept from.

"Roger," I said, pulling up beside the driver's side window. I puffed as if I were out of breath and acted surprised. "I thought you'd headed home to Connecticut." The binoculars hung from a strap around his neck and rested on his chest.

Angleford peered up at me, his eyes puffy and red.

"This is a difficult place to visit, isn't it?" I said.

With lips pressed tight together he nodded.

I had no idea what to say after that, so I squatted down next to the driver's door and the two of us simply watched the sun disappear behind the horizon the way a puppet drops off stage. We didn't speak for what felt like ten minutes, during which time half the cars in the parking lot left. I was about to invite him to dinner when he broke the silence.

"You don't really power-walk, do you, Dunc?" He looked slyly at me and I half-expected him to wink.

"No," I said.

"You were just watching over me, weren't you?"

"Yes."

"Well, I'm okay, Dunc. Really I am," he said. "You can go back to the inn now."

A new set of headlights drove into the park.

"Are they for enjoying the sunset, Roger?" I said, pointing to the binoculars.

"Take a look," Angleford said, pulling the strap

over his head and handing me his binoculars. He pointed at the lighthouse. "Focus on the catwalk."

I held the binoculars to my eyes and pointed them at the glass window panels around the lighthouse beacon. The light blinded me immediately, and I had to close my eyes.

"Oh, sorry, Dunc," Angleford said. "Watch out for the light. It comes around every five or six seconds. You'll learn to time it."

After a few rotations of the beacon I had the hang of it and squinted through the binoculars at the upper level of the white tower.

Damn!" I said. "Isn't that something? It really does look like giant moths."

Something—no, some things, shadowy things—appeared to be fluttering around up inside the glass-paneled lighthouse. Fluttering like moths caught under a jar. Or were they like moths attracted to a lamp?

"So what do you think, Dunc?" Angleford said. "Still betting they're giant shadows?"

Whether they were giant shadows or giant moths, I counted four of them bobbing and dancing up-and-down and side-to-side. When they caught the moonlight I realized they were translucent. Shadows weren't translucent. Shadows were projected onto something. What was I seeing?

I heard the car door open and turned to see Angleford climbing out. He stretched away his stiffness, then walked around and unlocked the car's trunk. He reached in and withdrew what looked like a set of pruning shears. Bolt cutters! Then he pulled out a small crow bar. He slammed the trunk shut and started across the dirt and gravel.

"Roger," I called in a half-whisper. "Where do you think you're going?"

He ignored my question and kept walking for the back of the Fisherman's Museum. I didn't want to follow him, but I couldn't help it.

"Wait for me, Roger," I called, and hurried after him.

By the time I caught up, Angleford had the crow bar wedged between the museum's back door and door frame.

"This is breaking and entering," I said, my words reminding me that I had always been a fraidy-cat in school. But with a loud crack the door popped open. In a moment we were in the back room of the museum, standing outside the padlocked door to the lighthouse itself. Angleford snapped on a disposable flashlight. So these were the things he had picked up in town earlier in the week—burglar's tools.

"The light switch is right here, Roger," I said, reaching for it. His strong hand gripped my wrist and held it.

"Don't," he said, shining the flashlight in my face. "I'm afraid it'll scare them."

Scare who? I wanted to say, but didn't. I was pretty sure I knew the answer.

"Hold the light," he said. A moment later the bolt cutters bit through the steel U of the padlock and Angleford pulled open the heavy door to the tower. The moonlight reflecting off the white inside walls revealed a set of wide stairs that spiraled around a center support up to the inner catwalk and beacon. Not needing the flashlight, Angleford led the way. We inched upward until Angleford halted me with a hand on the shoulder.

"Roger—" I started to say.

"Shhh," he whispered firmly, his fingers digging into my shoulder like a claw.

It was then that I heard them for the first time. *Whoosh-whoosh-whoosh. Whisk-whisk-whisk.* A soft fluttering like rustling silk, then like the wind breathing through fall foliage.

I tugged on Roger's belt. He turned and said quietly, "Stay here."

Before I could object, he slid onto the catwalk on his stomach and rolled slowly onto his back, inching farther around the circular walkway like a prisoner escaping under a fence. The full moon, a huge orange pendant now, seemed to be waiting and looking right into the lighthouse through the huge glass window panels. I crouched on the top stair.

There they were, four of them—rising, dipping, wobbling, weaving—not moths, but beings, like peanut-shaped soap bubbles, shimmery, wet-looking. I could see—both through them and inside them. It was like looking at a drop of water on a glass slide, except that these were two or three feet tall. Like embryos, I thought, it's like looking at a very pale, shadowy embryo in a sonogram.

Angleford lay on his back and raised his hands, then called, "Cara."

They began to move, no longer up and down, nor randomly, but purposefully, slowly organizing, getting in synch with one another, the four lighthouse moths. They moved sideways, the way the beacon rotated, circling slowly like horses in a carousel. They passed over Angleford, his hands passing through them. He kept calling "Cara. Cara. Cara."

They sped up—slowly, slowly, getting in step as if working together, creating a balance, the four of them like the four points of a compass or the wings on a windmill. They rose and sank and I heard a whine, a whine which, as they moved slowly, sounded like the night wind strumming the rope of a flagpole; then, as they circled faster, its pitch increased to the sound of summer's-end cicadas; and faster until they practically shrieked—Angleford all the time chanting Cara, Cara, Cara faster and faster—until finally they sang one note like the sound produced by rubbing a wetted finger around the rim of a crystal wineglass—just before it shatters. In trying to call Cara back, was Angleford agitating them?

He stopped calling her name, looked my way and said, "I know why I'm here now."

I plugged my ears. The moths circled the lens at incredible speed, yet they created no draft—only the ear-splitting note and a fine line of light that glowed like a hot filament wire in a toaster. Their movement had created something like a jet's vapor trail, except this wasn't straight or flat, but curved up and down ever so slightly like a sine wave. Was this as close to materializing as they could come?

Then he raised his hands again and called, "Cara, I love you. Cara, I love you. Cara, I love you." As he changed his chant, repeating this new one, they slowed down, slower, slower, until finally they rose and fell like a swelling sea, circling at the same speed as the rotating beacon. Their sound eased to a low, pleasant hum. Slow, rhythmic, peaceful. Calm, calm, calm.

Then the beacon's beam shone right through one of the moths, spotlighting it. It was like light shining through a soap bubble, and the moth, revolving in perfect synch with the light now, appeared to be resting, riding the beam. Was it the beacon, maybe the moonlight—I swear I caught a flash of flaming red—red what, red hair?

Angleford stood up, the revolving moths passing through him—or vice versa—as if he wasn't there. He approached the beacon and Roger Angleford reached in and clamped his hands around the burning hot bulb.

"Roger," I cried out, wincing. But I was helpless, frozen in place.

Angleford screamed, screamed but held on, held on as if his life depended on it. "Cara, I love you," he forced himself to utter one more time.

The moth in the light beam suddenly glowed bright, then burst. And as it burst, the full moon—I swear it looked like a laser—the huge smiling full moon hovering near the lighthouse shot forth a beam and drew the moth up to itself, called it home right through the plate glass window panel.

Angleford collapsed face-up on the catwalk in front of me, the stench of his seared flesh immediately assaulting my nostrils.

"Roger," I said, grabbing the front of his shirt and shaking. "Roger, are you all right?" I listened for his answer, but instead heard a fluttering above the catwalk. The other three moths, their balance upset by the departure of the other moth, had fallen out of synch. Something whooshed past me down the spiral staircase. Then another, and another. The lighthouse moths were gone, and I sat in silence, the beacon flashing in a slow circle above me.

I felt Angleford's neck for a pulse. None. The big man's chest didn't move. He wasn't breathing. I wanted to pound on it, breathe air into his mouth and lungs, but I knew he wouldn't want that.

As the bright orange moon shone in on us, I rested my hands on the body of Roger Angleford. I knew in that moment that I would deeply miss him. My heart hurt and I put my head down and began to weep.

"You were a good man, Roger," I said. "I love you."

Suddenly something, something peanut-shaped and translucent, not much bigger than a bag of groceries, bloomed from Roger's heart—bloomed in the way a soap bubble blooms to life from the bowl of a bubble pipe. It didn't rip his shirt or tear his skin. It simply appeared.

It rested a second, then brightened to a glow and burst. And as it burst, I felt a faint spray on my arms and face, a warm mist that felt like a light ocean spray on a warm summer evening. Then, as the first moth had done, this lighthouse moth shot out quietly through the window panel—drawn home to the bosom of the moon, leaving me by myself.

I walked home to the inn and phoned Bristol's First Responders, offering the more believable explanation that I had gone looking for a grief-stricken Angleford and, following my instincts, had eventually found his body up inside the lighthouse. I promised to return and meet them at the scene.

Then I dialed Suki Angleford. I recognized her by her accent as soon as she picked up. She sounded wide awake.

"Suki," I said, my throat tight. "It's about Cara—" Why did Cara pop out of my mouth when I meant Roger?

"Cara here," Suki said. "Gone now."

"Wait," I said, thinking Suki was preparing to hang up. "I meant to say Roger. He--"

"Here, too," she said. "Gone now," she repeated. "Cara fine. Roger fine. Thank you, Dunc." Suki hung up.

I don't recall if I whispered goodbye, but I remember even now the feel of her voice, how relaxed she sounded. Oddly, I felt that way, too--at peace.

A light breeze had come up, so I grabbed a windbreaker and stepped onto the porch. It was September first, and the evening air had that melancholy feel of approaching New England autumn. I set off toward the lighthouse, pale moonlight washing over the road and me and the leaves that would soon fall. As I walked down the center of the blacktop road, I could already hear around me the rustle and flutter—the rustle and flutter—of the leaves. Probably the leaves.

Garden Plot

"Garden Plot" calls to mind Perseus "facing" Medusa. But this story is also a cautionary tale about scoffing at others' beliefs. It appeared in *Green Mountain Trading Post*, April 22, 1992; *Beyond the Moon #4* (Second Prize, Horror), Winter 1994-95; *Splatter Effect*, December 1994; *All Hallows* (The Ghost Story Society, England), February 1995; *New Dawn Fades* (Scotland), Autumn 1995; *Peconic Bay Shopper*, October 1998; *Frightmares*, October 1998; *Goddess of the Bay*, December 1998; *Black Petals*, Spring 1999; *My Legacy* (Editor's Choice Award), November 2000. It was named Honorable Mention in *Year's Best Fantasy and Horror #9*, 1996.

I visited Vermont when I was ten. I'll never go back.

That was the summer I went to stay at Grampa Harder's farm. He lived in Bethel, out on the Back-Bethel Road that leads along the White River to Gaysville. Everybody called it the Injun Path, because there had been a couple of Indian settlements there around the time of the Revolution. Grampa said they were always turning up arrowheads in the fields after a hard rain or after plowing.

Every day I walked the two miles to town along the Injun Path, if not for the mail then for tobacco for Grampa.

A woman lived halfway between Grampa's and town. Folks said she was descended on the one side from the Abenaki Indians and on the other side from runaway slaves. She spent all her time tending a garden on the back corner of her property, a piece of river bottomland where the river oxbows and the land's shaped like a thumb. The garden had a low stone wall around it and a tall scarecrow in the middle. Grampa said every year that woman would shine up a couple of metal pie tins and hang them from the wrists of the scarecrow so the reflecting sun would scare off the crows. Nobody I talked to had ever seen her face.

I noticed when we drove by her place that no matter how hot it got, the old woman would always be dressed in dark clothes. She had a black veil—no, it was more of a hood—that covered her head so you couldn't see her face. Grampa said she was superstitious and wore it to ward off spirit-stealers, so they couldn't look her in the eye. That, Grampa said, was the only way they could possess you. Once they looked you directly in the eye, your soul belonged to them. Grampa also said spirit-stealers couldn't cross water.

A few months before I arrived, the Congregational Church hired a new minister, Reverend Evans. He made a lot of enemies in a short time. I sort of liked him, though. (My father died when I was young, and there weren't a lot of male figures in my life.) Reverend Evans was a character and, with that black suit and black broad-brimmed hat he wore, he could've played Ichabod Crane on stage.

I went to church with Grandma Harder most Sundays that summer, but Grampa only came along once. Grandma believed you should go whether you liked the minister or not, and always said, "Go to church through thick and thin, or heaven'll come and you'll not get in." Grampa disagreed and after one sitting under Reverend Evans' sharp tongue, he swore he'd never go back.

But it wasn't only the preaching that put Grampa

off. It was that Reverend Evans didn't take Grampa seriously. When Reverend Evans came to dinner, the two of them got into a discussion about souls, and Grampa brought up the spirit-stealers, saying that his father and grandfather had cautioned him about them. Reverend Evans pooh-poohed the notion, in the process belittling Grampa in front of Grandma and me. So, as if to issue a parting challenge when Reverend Evans left that night, Grampa said, "I'll tell you some-body who can give you an earful about spirit-stealers—the woman down the road. Why don't you stop by and chat with her some afternoon? Maybe you'll convert her."

Reverend Evans snorted back at Grampa, "I may just do that, Brother Harder. I do believe I may."

Two days later I was walking to town. When I passed the old woman's place, I could see her standing out near the back of her property, by the bow in the river, her regular black outfit on, bent over her garden. I could make out the scarecrow with its broad-brimmed straw hat, red plaid shirt, and black pants. Two pie tins hung from its wrists, glints of sun rico-chetting off them.

Now who should come walking up the road but Reverend Evans in his minister's suit and hat. We talked beside the road for a minute, and he said he was going to see the old woman. I told him I'd seen her in her garden, then I went on toward town.

It was late afternoon when I started for home. Still plenty of sunlight, but I'd have to hustle to get back in time for supper. I approached the old woman's place and saw she was still out there, bent over, weeding. At first I thought nothing of it, then a feeling came over me like a cold breeze on the back of my neck. I looked behind me. No breeze and no one watching.

Something was wrong. When I turned to look at

the woman, she was gone. Had she collapsed in the garden? I squinted but still couldn't make her out, so I walked fast toward the stone wall. I still couldn't see her, and broke into a run, scared I'd find her dead and scared to death I'd find her alive. I stopped at the wall. She had to be inside. There was no gate. Something—dread—stopped me from climbing over the wall. It was waist high, so I looked over it.

It wasn't just a garden. Mixed with the snap-peas and knee-high corn were stones, markers with faded writing on them. A bone yard. A burial ground. She was tending a grave garden. The cold chill pricked my neck again.

I glimpsed a movement to the right—sensed as much as saw it—something black and fast ducking behind the corn. Then a rustling, but not the wind. Water. Rippling. The river. The sound brought me back to myself.

Something moved. I glanced at the scarecrow and, my God, it wasn't wearing its usual broad-brimmed hat—now the hat was black. I looked into its face and, my God, it was Reverend Evans, eyes popped wide, mouth gaped as if trying to scream a warning. But no sound came out.

Suddenly I glimpsed a reflection in the pie tin on the scarecrow's arm. A head. In a hood. No face. More like oil on pond scum. She was behind me. Her icy breath pricked my neck, and the odor of rotten cheese invaded my nostrils. I shut my eyes and held my breath to keep from vomiting, and as I did, Grampa Harder's warning came back to me. If I turned around, she'd have me.

I sighted in on the water, shut my eyes tightly, and lit out for the river—leaping, sobbing, swatting at the back of my neck, all the while shouting out a prayer, "Now I lay me down to sleep; now I lay me down to

GARDEN PLOT

sleep . . .." With who-knows-what riding my shoulders and chewing my neck, I plunged in darkness through the reeds and clawed my way across the shallows, cutting and scratching my knees. Finally, deep water. I stayed under longer than I ever have, and let the current carry me downstream, coming up only a few times for air, always eyes clamped shut. I felt and floated my way downriver to town, and when I climbed onto shore near the town bridge, whatever had been on my back was gone.

I have no idea what happened to Reverend Evans. The constable couldn't find him. Grandma said he had likely left town before the church could ask him to resign. As for me, I begged so hard to go home that Grampa put me on a train early the next morning.

I haven't been to Vermont since, or even to the country, for that matter. My nerves wouldn't take it. At least here in the city I feel somewhat safe. Even so, though, if I see a bag lady coming down the sidewalk with a scarf over her head, I'll cross the street to avoid her. Just the thought of having to look her in the face gives me the creeps.

The Mason's Leech

"The Mason's Leech" creates a new urban legend, an odd and original variation on vampirism. It appeared in *Midnight Never Comes* (Christopher and Barbara Roden, editors, 1997), the acclaimed hardcover anthology from World Fantasy Award-winning Ash-Tree Press. Horror reviewer Stefan Dziemianowicz, in a review of the anthology for All Hallows: The Journal of The Ghost Story Society (Vol. 17, February 1998), wrote: "I have a weakness for stories that verge on the gruesome, which may explain my enjoyment of Steve Burt's 'The Mason's Leech.' I don't know if there is any truth to the primitive practice of walling up animals alive to help mortar dry faster, but Burt's story successfully suspended my disbelief in it and is a fine example of how discreet handling of distasteful subject matter can be used to convey an indirect sense of physical horror." The story also appeared in *Beyond the Moon* (First Prize, Horror), Fall 1994; *Peconic Bay Shopper*, October 1994 and October 1998; *In Vein*, April 1995; *Goddess of the Bay #4*, October 1998; *Lincoln County Weekly*, August 6, 1998; *Black Petals*, June 1999; *My Legacy*, February 2000; *Black Rose* (Ireland), July 2000; *Nocturnal Lyric #58*, January 2001. Horror editor Ellen Datlow named it Honorable Mention in *Year's Best Fantasy and Horror #11*, 1998.

It started when the demolition crew began knocking down the old nail factory around the corner. The factory's been empty for years, decades maybe, and except for being a spooky place for the kids to play in, it's just an eyesore. It quit operating as a nail factory back before Shook and me got into high school, and we been out of school for two years now.

We were down there, me and Shook, sitting on a rock wall that runs the back boundary of the nail factory property. We were like little kids, watching the backhoe and the bulldozer and the wrecking ball that swings from the boom of the crane.

All of a sudden things stopped and the demolition crew crowded around this hole in a section of wall that'd been giving them trouble. The concrete was like iron, super hard, much harder than any other part of the building walls. From a distance we guessed it was three or four feet thick. But one of the workers yelled out, "I think it's hollow." A half dozen hard hats closed in and huddled in front of the hole the wrecking ball had pounded. Two of them whacked at it with sledge hammers and two others started in with six-foot pry bars.

Me and Shook walked over for a closer look.

"Hook onto it with that dump truck," one of the hard hats yelled, so the driver backed in close and ran a cable from the trailer hitch around the wall and back onto the hitch. Easy as pie, the truck pulled the wall section—must've been ten foot by twenty foot—whump—right over onto the ground in front of us. Everybody stood there dead quiet, staring into the wall.

"What the hell's that?" Shook said.

"Looks like a dead fox," I said.

"Or a dog," one of the hard hats said.

"It's a pup," Shook said. "A German Shepherd." He stepped closer in for a better look. "About six months, I'd guess." Shook had owned a German Shepherd when we were growing up. It had been killed by a car one day when Shook was supposed to be watching it and it got away from him.

"How come it's not rotten?" a hard hat said. "It's been in that wall a lot of years."

"No air," somebody said. "Like a mummy in a pyramid."

"Looks better'n any mummy I ever seen," Shook said.

To me it just looked like it was asleep, except that it'd been sealed in that wall for fifty or so years.

"So how'd it get in the wall?" somebody asked.

"Accident," the truck driver said. As he said the words, Shook reached toward the pup.

"Don't!" someone yelled. Shook pulled back like he'd leaned on a hot stove. It was the foreman who yelled.

"It's not an accident," he said. "Look at its tongue."

Everybody looked. It reminded me of a kid licking an ice cube tray. Its tongue was stuck, attached to the concrete wall.

"It's a mason's leech," the foreman said.

The hard hats looked at each other and whispered among themselves. Then they backed away from Shook and the pup.

"What's a mason's leech?" I asked.

The foreman looked at me, his face cloudy. "Everybody who's worked with concrete has heard of mason's leeches," he said. "Until today, though, even I'd thought it was a myth. And I've been in this business thirty-seven years. This is the first one I've ever seen."

I tried to read the faces of the foreman and the others to see if they were putting us on. Their faces gave away nothing. They looked dead serious.

"Heck, till now we all figured it was a myth, didn't we, men?" the foreman asked. The hard hats nodded. "But this—this is bad news."

"But why?" I asked. "It's just a dead dog, isn't it?"

"I'll tell you what my grandfather told me. He was a stonemason. Concrete takes a long time to dry all the way through. Thirteen years, they say. But, just like us, masons fifty years ago had deadlines. So, to dry a concrete wall faster, they'd take a puppy, infect it with cholera, and put it in a wall and seal it up. Called it a mason's leech. The cholera'd give it awful diarrhea so it'd get dehydrated in no time. That'd make it thirsty as hell, so thirsty it'd attach its tongue to the concrete and try to suck all the moisture out, like a sponge drawing water into itself. That thing there, I believe, is a mason's leech."

I looked at the dog with its tongue stuck to the concrete, then looked again to see if any of the hard hats were smiling. No one smiled.

"Is it true?" I asked the foreman. "Can it be?"

He shrugged. "Don't know. My grandfather said they quit doing it in the thirties when a whole crew came down with cholera and died."

I knew my mouth was hanging wide open, but I couldn't do anything about it.

"Hell," Shook said abruptly. "Somebody's got to bury it." He reached under the pup to pick it up.

"Don't touch it," the foreman yelled. A chill ran down my back. I wondered if the germs could still be alive after fifty years in a tomb.

"That's it!" the foreman yelled. "Pack up, men. We're outta here." He waved his arms like a drill sergeant ordering soldiers into a troop truck. They dropped their tools and in less than two minutes were driving away.

"Hey!" Shook yelled at me. "Get a shovel."

I turned to look, and there, beside the collapsed wall, stood Shook, the dog balanced on his upturned palms. I didn't ask how he got the tongue loose.

"Shook," I said. "Didn't you hear the man? Cholera."

"Oh, sure. Right. Cholera. You believe that crap?"

I hated it when Shook did that, made me feel stupid. "Look," I said, "I know it's far-fetched. But the man

seemed convinced, damned convinced. And didn't they all scatter fast? You think they'd take that much trouble for a joke?"

Shook's lip curled in a doubter's smile.

"Hey," I said, "Even if it's not true about sucking the wall, even if that's crap, it's still possible the dog's diseased, ain't it?"

Shook stared at me as if I was an idiot, then laughed. I didn't laugh with him. I was worried. Then, holding the dog as if offering some strange sacrifice, he said, "Hey, this dog's warm."

I looked at him, waiting for him to say April Fool. But he didn't. And he didn't drop it. He said, "Here. Feel it," and held the carcass toward me. I shied back.

"I'm serious," he said. "It's warm, almost like it's alive. C'mon, feel it."

I don't know why he didn't drop it then. I was a nervous wreck. But the pup really did look like any-body's regular old pet asleep on a porch. So I put out my fingers towards its flank—to show Shook I wasn't scared, not because I wanted to. I don't know if I was more afraid of it feeling cold or feeling warm. I flinched when he pressed it against my fingertips. I wondered if germs could jump like fleas.

"It is warm," I said, disbelieving my own words.

"Told you," Shook said. "Getting warmer all the time."

I looked around at the road to see if anyone else might verify it.

"Damn, it's breathing," Shook said.

I snapped around, not believing my ears.

"Look at its side," he said. "It really is breathing."

It did look like it was breathing, but I tried to convince myself and Shook otherwise. "That's your hands shaking," I said. "That's what's doing it."

Shook looked me straight in the eye. "It's not me," he said, licking his lips nervously. "The frigging dog is breathing. It's alive."

I glanced at the pup's face. Its eyelid was half open. That's when I noticed the layer of skin from the top of its tongue was gone, no doubt still attached to the wall. But what was odd was that its tongue, despite the missing skin, was moist. Its black nose seemed to glisten with moisture; but from where?

My heart leaped as I felt the terror rising in me.

"This dog's not dead," Shook blurted, a funny smile on his face. "Really, it's alive."

Shook had to be confused, although I wasn't sure of anything myself at that moment. One thing I did know—that dog wasn't alive ten minutes earlier. It was dead. For fifty years.

"Oh, look," Shook said, wetting his lips with his tongue again. He looked tired, pale. "The puppy moved its head." He sounded like a kid oohing over a cute Christmas gift.

I looked back to the pup. Its eyes were fully open, moist, and it strained to raise its head the way an old dog on its deathbed does.

Shook's arms trembled, tired from holding the dog on his palms. He pulled it to his chest, cradling it on his forearms the way he might a child. He gazed down into its eyes and for a second I thought, "This is amazing; this really is a cute puppy."

Then it snapped at Shook's face, gluing its tongue to his lips. Shook yanked his hands from under it, but the dog hung from his mouth by its tongue.

Shook looked at me, his face a mask of horror. His eyes pleaded, "Help me," but no sounds came from his mouth. He could only grunt. He leaned forward, pulled down by the dog's weight, frantically trying to pull the dog off his face. But it was hopeless, like an elephant trying to remove its own trunk.

I ran. It's the only thing I could do. I deserted my best friend Shook, left him kissing a dog from hell that wanted to suck the moisture and life out of him the way it dried concrete. I ran home and hid in my room for two days.

Finally the cops showed up, wanting to ask questions. They'd found Shook's body at the demolition site, his skin black as a rotten banana peel and barely hanging on the bones. *Deflated* was the word one of the cops used. *Crushed,* the other said, collapsed like a beer can with the air sucked out of it.

I told them what I saw, but no dog was found. Tracks leading away from Shook's body, yes, dog tracks. But no dog. The story, they say, is far-fetched, but they have no other possibilities.

So now I go from the house to the car to the store, then back, making sure I'm out in the open as little as possible. I spend most of my time inside, with the doors locked, because when I'm out, I'm afraid I'll turn and it'll be on me, snarling and sucking, going for my mouth.

Maybe the worst is the night. I wash my hands a hundred times a day now, and I get up almost as many times to do it at night—because I touched it, I touched it on its breathing, friggin' flank. Shook made me touch it! And I don't know if I'll get whatever it had. All I know tonight is, the more I lie here and wonder, the thirstier I get. The thirstier I get, and I hope to God it's only my imagination.

The Strand

"The Strand" brings together an American Gothic setting, the Maine coast, and a narrative reminiscent of the stories of M.R. James, one of the grand-daddies of British supernatural fiction. The story appeared in *Dread*, April 2000, then in *Threshold*, Fall 2000. It was named Honorable Mention in *Year's Best Fantasy and Horror #14*, 2001.

Each summer from age nine to fifteen I traveled to Maine and stayed a week with my great-aunt Victoria at Ocean House, her twenty-room "cottage" on the Nubble. Widowed early when her husband Archibald's plane went down in the Atlantic, she was incredibly wealthy.

As I got off the train for my fourth vacation—just turned twelve—something occurred to me. I knew where I would find Aunt Victoria. I knew what she'd be doing when I got to Ocean House. Alfred, her only resident servant, would meet me, offer his stiff, formal handshake, and tell me Aunt Victoria was in the parlor and I'd have to wait until dinnertime to greet her. Which meant, I then saw, that Aunt Victoria was in the parlor in gown and pearls—never without a strand of pearls about her neck—entertaining a new suitor. It had been so my first three visits, and it would be so that year and each year thereafter.

At the end of my seventh stay, the summer I turned fifteen, I knew I could never return there again.

The first year I was met at the train by Alfred, who had been my aunt's manservant for thirty years, since shortly before she was widowed. After collecting me at the station, Alfred gave me a walking tour of the harbor town, pointing out the places a boy needed to know about—Post Office, candy store, Harbor Cafe, and the boarding house (if bad weather prevented my reaching Ocean House). He asked the questions adults feel obliged to ask. What grade are you in? How do you like school? Has your summer vacation been enjoyable? I could see Alfred wasn't comfortable with children. He was polite but not enthused.

Alfred seemed distracted. He checked his pocket watch often. Finally he tugged the watch from his pocket and pronounced, "Close enough. Let's go, Master Robert."

Off we traipsed, walking a worn dirt path away from town, beneath a canopy of tall pine trees, then among shorter, scrubbier ones. For more than a half mile we picked our way among rock outcroppings until we emerged onto a bluff with a breathtaking ocean vista. Not a ship or island in sight, nothing but bobbing gulls and lobster buoys riding easy swells. Before I could absorb it, Alfred interrupted.

"The Nubble," he declared, motioning downcoast. "Ocean House at the center."

There in the distance, a half mile from us but barely two hundred yards offshore, loomed an island. I didn't recognize it as an island at first, because it blended into the curve of coastline behind it. But once Alfred pointed it out, I could see it was indeed separate from the mainland. Ocean House, built on a hill and embraced by the island's gray rock-ribbed perimeter, looked like a weathered castle.

"But there's no drawbridge, Alfred," I said. "How do we get out to it? Boat?"

"There," he said, pointing to a strip of dark gray running between the blue-green water of the seaward side and the blackish water of the mainland side.

"A sand bar?" I asked.

"The Strand. A natural bridge of sorts, a ledge of rock exposed by the glacier. Up close you'll see gouges and stripes, like giant claw marks. It connects the Nubble with the mainland."

"But it's underwater," I said.

"Yes, most of the time. When tides are normal it's passable two hours before low tide and two hours after. By the time we get down there, it'll be almost dry enough to cross."

Fifteen minutes later we stood on the shore of the mainland among pink and purple beach roses. We were ahead of schedule and I could see the waters draining back from the Strand. In the twenty minutes we waited for it to become crossable, Alfred told me what I needed to know about the Strand, the Nubble, Ocean House, and Aunt Victoria.

I'd never met Aunt Victoria before, and our getting acquainted over dinner was awkward. It may have been due to her lack of experience conversing with nine year-old boys, but it was also largely due to the attention she accorded her dinner guest, Mr. Belden, the suitor from the parlor. But if Aunt Victoria neglected me in conversation, Mr. Belden worked to include me.

"So, how do you like school, Robert?"

"Fine."

"Favorite subjects?"

"History and Reading."

"Like sports?"

"I love baseball, and I'm learning to play basketball."

"Planning to fish while you're here?"

"Don't know. I've never fished in the ocean, only in ponds and streams back home. Who would take me?"

"Well, that's the great thing about fishing—if you know how to fish, you can go by yourself. It's not a team sport; you can do it alone."

I must have perked up at that, because Mr. Belden picked up a clam on the halfshell and said, "And there's clamming. Another activity you can do alone. Why, I'll bet at low tide it's great clamming along those mud flats inside the Str—"

"Absolutely not!" Aunt Victoria piped. "Mr. Belden! The boy will stay away from those flats. A rising tide could catch him with his feet in that muck and drown him."

Then to me, "The Strand is for crossing, young man. And that's all—crossing. Understand?"

I spent most of the week either exploring the Nubble or learning my way around town. Whenever I crossed the Strand either direction, I heeded my aunt's stern warning, picking my way quickly across as if running a gauntlet. Something about her voice had frightened me deeply. She'd created an image I couldn't shake, a mental picture that began to appear as a nightmare, of myself mired in the black mud flats, gasping upward as waves lapped in and the tide inched above my mouth and nose. The first few crossings I ran like the wind.

It was week's end before I ran into Mr. Belden again. "Thank you, Victoria, for your gracious hospitality," I heard him say as the parlor door opened. "I hope you'll give my proposal serious consideration."

I didn't know if his word—proposal—described a business deal or an offer of marriage. But the image that sprang to mind was Mr. Belden on bended knee looking pleadingly up into my aunt's eyes, her hand resting on his as he popped the question. Had he made the offer in the old-fashioned way, with a diamond ring? Or had Mr. Belden been astute enough to break tradition and present a worthy pearl?

In the twelve months following, no wedding announcement came.

Over the years suitors flocked to the Nubble like geese to grain, including a dashing black-haired Frenchman named Guy LeFochaud, a widowed Maine lumber baron named Dearstyne, and an eligible bachelor named Dr. Toffler, who had retired from a New York City hospital. No wedding plans ever came after the visits, though. Was romance a game my aunt played, or was there simply no suitable candidate, no man who lit her up the way her dear departed Archie had?

That first year was the only year anyone met my train. After that I was on my own, the path between town and Ocean House quickly becoming so familiar that there was no need for anyone to accompany me. Beginning my second year, I arrived by train alone, lugged my suitcase through the pine barrens alone, negotiated the Strand alone.

After the first year, as my confidence grew, my crossings of the Strand became more leisurely. I explored the sand apron along the ocean side. I played tag with the waves and timed my crossings closer and closer. One day in my second or third year I got briefly stranded on a boulder midway across. I quickly realized the water would only get higher and I had little choice but to get wet. I ripped off my shoes and slogged the rest of the way, the water at my knees by the time I climbed onto the Nubble. I had beaten it. I sat on the grass, victorious. But then the picture which always hung in the background of my mind—the gasping boy with water filling his mouth—flashed in my head and made me shudder. I had beaten it—*this time.*

My fifth year I climbed off the train as a nor'easter hit, forcing me to take lodging in town. The storm blew itself out overnight. Next morning as I sat eating my breakfast at the Harbor Cafe, I heard everyone jabbering about storm damage—trees down, power lost, boats beached, lobster traps smashed on the rocks, tons of seaweed washed ashore. The storm's fury had touched not only what we could see—land, air, water's surface—but it had also churned up what lay beneath.

When I got to the Strand that morning, even though the tidetables listed dead low tide as nine-fifteen, several feet of tidal water covered the rock pathway and angry whitecaps washed rhythmically over it. The storm had created higher than normal tides and the Strand was impassable. I either had to stay another night and try again next morning or I could wait ten or twelve hours for the next low tide, just before dark.

A half-hour before sunset I returned from town and pulled my suitcase from its hiding place in the pines. The full moon was rising even as the sun settled toward the horizon, and the waters covering the Strand weren't deeper than a foot in most places. It would be dry in less than half an hour, so I sat on my suitcase to wait, certain I'd be able to cross in the moonlight.

Something caught my eye way off in the mud flats, close to the Nubble. It looked like a person, thigh-deep or even waist-deep in the water, bending over, then straightening up again and again. With both sunlight and moonlight playing tricks on the water it was difficult to see clearly, but I felt certain it was a man clamming. If someone could clam, I could cross.

I picked up my bag and clambered down to the beach. The Strand's first fifty yards glistened with moisture but it was dry enough to walk on. Part of the crossing, though, would require wading, so I removed my shoes and trousers, stuffed them in the suitcase, and stood shivering in my undershorts.

The sun had slid halfway over the horizon so that between the shadows and the distance I still couldn't clearly make out the clammer. Was Aunt Victoria aware of it? How long had this been going on?

I slung my suitcase under my shoulder and set out. My bare feet slipped on the cold wet strands of seaweed the storm had dumped across the travel surface. Fifty yards along I saw a tangled wire cage, a lobster trap, dashed on the rocks. Near it lay a clot of buoys on a snapped-off tether. The nor'easter had stirred up the ocean bottom and driven ashore plenty of debris. I stopped in puddles of chilly water, and by the time I came to the place where I'd have to begin wading, my feet were already numb. There was almost no wave action now, only a gentle licking, and I was sure if I stayed on the Strand's main path it would get no deeper than my knees. I switched the suitcase to the other shoulder and waded in, ankles aching as soon as the icy waters closed around them. I'd forgotten how cold Maine waters were, even in summer.

The sun disappeared and the area around me was suddenly bathed in moonlight. Trouble was, I couldn't see below the surface, and the path was no longer visible. I had to feel my way with my feet, try to sight in on the Nubble and work from memory. At least the water was receding, and soon I'd see the dry portion of the path at the Nubble end.

Suddenly it grew dark, a fleece of clouds over the moon. I froze in place, unsure of my bearings, afraid to slip and fall. I dared not move forward without some marker.

A flashlight snapped on, the clammer not far off.

"Hullo!" I yelled, and the beam swung in my direction. "Can you help me?"

The flashlight moved toward me.

"Master Robert?"

"Alfred?"

I was never so glad to see anyone. In less than a minute Alfred, clad in chest-high rubber waders, was taking the suitcase from my shoulder and walking methe rest of the way across the Strand.

"What were you doing out there, Alfred?" I asked once we were on dry ground. "I thought you were a clammer."

"Clamming? No clams along the Strand," he said. "Checking for storm damage. I was just preparing to come in."

Then he chuckled.

"What?" I said, shivering in the cool air.

"Perhaps you should remain here a moment before greeting your aunt," he said, setting my suitcase down on the grass and patting it. "I trust your trousers, socks, and shoes are in here. I'll go tell her you've arrived safely." And off he waddled in the waders.

That year the man who stayed at Ocean House during my week wasn't a suitor. He visited only two days, and his business with Aunt Victoria seemed to be just exactly that—business. He was Eli Goldman, a New York City jeweler. He arrived with a trunk containing more than a hundred tiny compartments, each housing felt-lined jewelry cases. For two solid days—with the exception of polite conversation at meals—he and my aunt spoke of nothing but pearls and settings.

One afternoon I walked in on them in the dining room and saw tables laden with necklaces, rings, bracelets, watches, brooches, and near Aunt Victoria, bowls of loose pearls that looked like breakfast cereal awaiting milk. One bowl held pearls the size of golf balls.

"Let me show you *these*," Aunt Victoria said, and reached into a huge cloth knitting bag. She withdrew a pearl the size of a bowling ball, waited for Goldman to gasp, then produced another, slightly larger, and when he was totally speechless and wide-eyed, pulled out a third the size of a basketball. She set them on the table and let the jeweler examine them.

"Unbelievable," he said, shaking his head again

and again. "I've never seen anything like these. Not even from the South Seas. How do you get them so large?" (Not *where*, I remember now, but *how*.)

"Special culture," Aunt Victoria said. "Special culture."

I had no idea whether my aunt was buying pearls, selling pearls, or selecting settings.

The seventh summer, my last, I finally dared to ask Alfred, "Do you think the right man will ever come along again for Aunt Victoria?"

"Who can say?" he shrugged. "Maybe this summer. Maybe next. Come inside and meet Professor Cassiday."

Professor Cassiday was a retired university educator from the Midwest. The first thing that struck me about him was his bulbous red nose, which reminded me of W.C. Fields and Karl Malden. With his bushy eyebrows, Cassiday more resembled Malden. He seemed quite smitten with my aunt, gallantly kissing her hand every time they met. I wondered if he'd be the one.

On my final night at Ocean House I was startled awake by the awful nightmare about the mud flats. I hadn't suffered it in two years. But I knew I'd been gasping in my sleep. My throat was sandpapery, my mouth cottony. I padded toward the kitchen for a glass of milk. As I tiptoed past my aunt's bedroom I heard giggling and laughter, one voice my aunt's, the other voice a man's. I hesitated in the hallway, wondering if Cassiday and my aunt were engaged in a romantic interlude. It was difficult to imagine the thick-browed professor nuzzling Aunt Victoria with that huge red nose.

"That was wonderful," I heard her say. "You make me feel young."

"My pleasure," the man said. "Always."

The voice wasn't Cassiday's. It was Alfred's. I tiptoed quickly back to my room and climbed back into bed.

The next morning, after Alfred served breakfast to Professor Cassiday, Aunt Victoria, and me, I said my goodbyes. My train wasn't until after noontime, but I wanted to get going. Low tide came around eleven, which meant the Strand was crossable between nine and one. I was eager to leave. I couldn't look Aunt Victoria or Alfred in the eye.

I spent the morning roaming around town, and at noon found myself in the Harbor Cafe preparing to order lunch.

"So," said the waitress. "How many more days before you go home, Robert?"

"About two hours from now," I said.

"No suitcase?" she asked.

I looked beside my chair. No suitcase. Where had I left it? Not at the train station. Not along the path. I didn't recall lugging it across the Strand. Damn! I had stopped on the downhill between Ocean House and the Strand and sat on a boulder to tie my shoe. I'd set the suitcase in the shadow of the boulder, where it still sat.

I bolted out of the cafe, knowing I barely had time to catch the Strand dry both ways. I would sprint across, grab the bag, and sprint back. If I could make the Strand, catching the train wouldn't be a problem.

The gauntlet was fifteen feet wide when I reached it, the waters closing. I hurried, knowing the return trip would be slower with the suitcase. But the ruts hampered me—I couldn't risk twisting an ankle—so I picked my way across as nimbly as I could.

Midway across I looked toward Ocean House to catch my bearings, and out of the corner of my eye saw a movement on the mud flats, a figure bent over at the waist in the water—almost the same scene as the evening I'd spotted Alfred checking for storm damage, except that now he had an inner tube with a basket set in it tethered to his waist. But I saw no clam rake.

"Alfred? Is that you?" I cried.

The man straightened, looked my way.

"Master Robert?" Alfred called. He had on the chest-high rubber waders. "Don't come—" he started to say once he recognized me. But as the words left his mouth, he stumbled and had to struggle to regain his balance. I couldn't help reacting—I was afraid he'd fall—so I stepped toward him, prepared to wade in if necessary.

"No!" he barked as he straightened up. "No!"

"But Alfred," I said, wanting to tell him I was only trying to help if he needed it.

Alfred saw me looking toward the inner tube and basket. Something about his eyes changed in that instant, as if he were making a mental shift, a decision. But I failed to sense the rising menace in his voice.

"Master Robert, come here," he said, more ordering than cajoling. "Come closer."

"My clothes," I said, something inside telling me to resist. "They'll get wet." His request made no sense. He had recovered his balance.

"My foot," he said. "It's— It's stuck."

I saw something in his eyes then, the first hint of what—pain? Or something else—a sudden idea, a new ploy? He put his hand to his chest and grimaced.

"Master Robert, come quickly," he pleaded. "My heart."

And before I could think, I clambered into the water and slogged toward him.

"Hold on, Alfred," I called. "I'm coming."

I reached him in moments, and as I did he suddenly straightened to his full height, jaw tight, eyes bulging. He clamped his hands on my shoulders and pressed down.

"What? Alfred! No!" I cried.

But his strong arms pushed me under and held me down. I struggled against him, but I had no leverage for my hands, no purchase on the muddy bottom for my feet. My mouth opened for air and instead took in a gulp of sea water, which for a moment had an oddly calming effect. I relaxed, either growing weaker or resigned. My eyes opened and I found myself staring directly into a huge open oyster shell, a shell the size of a Revolutionary War tombstone, and from the center of it someone stared back, grinning lifelessly. *It was a head*—no body—just a head in the oyster shell, as if it were the mollusk itself.

In my terror I flailed my arms and grabbed at the only thing I could reach—the chest of Alfred's rubber waders—and pulled down. Sea water spilled in and I felt him pitch forward in the water. He released his grip on me as he fought to keep his own head above water. I pushed out from under him and burst to the surface, greedily sucking down breaths of air.

Alfred floated almost flat for a moment, head craned up for air, hand stretched toward me for help. But then the water completely filled the waders and he sank beneath the surface. Part of me wanted to save him, but then I glanced at the inner tube tied to him. Gaping up at me from the basket in the tube was a face, a face whose bushy eyebrows and bulbous nose I recognized. I tried to push the tube away from me, but it was tethered to Alfred and wouldn't go away. I scrambled for the Strand, half-running and half-swimming, vomiting sea water and lunch as I went. The Nubble was closer than the mainland, but I ran for town.

An hour later, weak and shivering in a police car, I told a Trooper my story. And while I called my mother from the Harbor Cafe, more police arrived and they started the investigation. But by the time anyone could get down to the Strand, the tide had come in, and things didn't get into full swing for another eight hours. They did manage to get a boat out, though, and found the inner tube with Cassiday's head in its basket and Alfred's body anchored below. They couldn't check out the mud flats then, but they did drop a marker buoy. Then they beached the boat on the Nubble and walked up to Ocean House to tell Aunt Victoria about Alfred. She broke down and cried.

The next morning, while I waited for my mother to arrive in Maine with the car to drive me home, police divers found the giant shells, five of them. Each was between three and four feet from hinge to tip. They dug them out of the mud flat, brought them ashore, and opened them. The shells actually contained live oysters. And in the mouths of four of them were nested four huge pearls, the pearls varying in size from that of a bowling ball to that of a good-sized pumpkin. The fifth oyster, they said, contained not a pearl, *but a head,* with a thin, almost caramel-like coating around it. The oyster hadn't yet had enough time to spin much substance around its irritant, so the veil was thin. That's when they asked me to look and see if I could identify the victim. That face that grinned through was Dr. Toffler's.

They cracked open the other pearls and found heads entombed in them as well. Black-haired Guy LeFochaud, Mr. Dearstyne, a man I didn't recognize, and Mr. Belden, who had shown me a clam on the half-shell. Seeing them that way turned my stomach. I was never so glad to return home as I was after that. Thank God they didn't call me to come back.

Eleven decapitated bodies were dug up on the Nubble that summer. Aunt Victoria still had two huge pearls in her possession, apparently having sold or otherwise disposed of several others over the years. She cooperated in surrendering the remaining two to authorities. The smaller of the two, when smashed, contained another unidentifiable head (at least Aunt Victoria wouldn't identify the man). And the larger of the two, by far the largest of all the pearls, the pride of her collection, when cracked, yielded Archie, Aunt Victoria's late husband.

Aunt Victoria admitted Alfred had been her lover for many years—a lover who presented her with fabulous pearls quite regularly, yet a lover it would have been beneath her station to marry. She denied any complicity in Alfred's crimes or any knowledge at all. She had had no idea where the pearls came from, she said, and didn't ask.

"It would have been impolite," she said.

And when questioned about the men who disappeared, she explained that Alfred must have murdered them after they had made their goodbyes and headed for the mainland.

"Alfred usually escorted them to the train," she said. "I always wondered why they never came back the next summer."

I never went back to the Nubble and I never again made contact with my aunt, who married Eli Goldman, the New York jeweler, two years later, and died a decade later.

But even now, one or two nights every summer, always during the week I visited Maine, I suffer the nightmare. Except it's a variation on those I had back then. Now I wake up gasping, mouth dry, sandpapery, and I gag—always gag—because I find my tongue curled around a firm little wad of mucus and hair. I get out of bed, dry heaving as I go, and stumble to the toilet, where I spit again and again until the wad is out. I flush it away and—irrational as it is—brush my teeth and rinse my mouth three, four, five times. I can't help it. I have to get rid of it, the wad in my mouth, and the taste, that bitter, choking taste of salt water.

And then I sit up awhile, fretting, wondering if I should have mentioned to the police my aunt's comment to Goldman the day she showed him the huge pearls. I ask myself how much she might really have known, while her voice echoes in my ears: "Special culture. Special culture."

Casino Night

"Casino Night" isn't a ghost story, but it's haunting, disturbing. Set in the not too distant future, it's an odd little cautionary tale encompassing various horrors. The story appeared in England's *Psychotrope* (Spring 2000), then in *Black Petals* (Autumn 2000). It earned an Honorable Mention in *Year's Best Fantasy & Horror 14*, August 2001.

So stop me if you've heard this one. A minister, a priest, and a rabbi are standing in a parking lot, standing as if in some weird prayer circle and holding onto what looks like a giant hula hoop that's got something like a skin stretched tightly across it. They're swaying from side to side, here and there, like drunken sailors, eyes lifted heavenward.

You haven't heard it? I thought you had, from the lack of attention you're paying the story. Maybe if I come at it another way.

A man in a powder blue suit gets out of an elevator at the Tenth Floor of a ten-story building, then enters the stairwell and climbs the steps to the roof. He pauses, shaking his head in astonishment at first, then smiles. The roof's decked out like a Hawaian luau—Japanese lanterns, festive ferns and potted rubber trees all around, a waterfall and pool in the center. Smiling waiters carry drinks on small round trays and waitresses circulate through the crowds with platters of hot and cold hors d'ouevres. Everything's free to Guests. Some of the Guests laugh and smile, others look deadly serious, some seem tense and anxious.

"Welcome to Casino Night, sir," a tuxedoed blonde says to the man in the powder blue suit. "If you'd please sign in."

She stands next to a short lectern like ministers use for their notes when preaching in funeral homes, points to the guest register on it. A placard is taped to the front of the lectern (Must Be Clearly Posted, it says in small print), its three-inch black letters displaying a fifteen-digit Government Registry Number. This is a duly authorized Casino Night, not unlike the twentieth century's old neighborhood Sports Bar. The expiration date is printed below the Government Registry Number—2010—two years before the gaming license has to be renewed.

"Remember, sir," the tuxedoed blonde says. "Two signatures." He glances up at her and she smiles one of those just-doing-my-duty smiles and says, "It's the law."

There are spaces for two signatures next to each other: Guest and Verifier. The man looks up imploringly at the blonde.

"Sorry, sir," she says. "You know I can't verify. I work here."

The man's face registers mild disappointment. He knows he won't have to wait long, but it's an annoying formality.

"Oh, someone's coming up the stairs now," the blonde says perkily.

A man in a red turtleneck steps from the stairway up into the night air.

"Lovely night," he says to no one in particular. "Warm, dry, plenty of stars. A perfect night."

The blonde pouts her lips and echoes his words, "Mmm, perfect night, perfect."

The man in the red turtleneck looks at the man in the powder blue suit and says, "I sign for you, you sign for me?"

Powder blue nods. It doesn't matter that they don't know each other, have never laid eyes on one another. The government's only requirement is that Casino Night Guests sign in, testifying they're over eighteen, and that someone witnesses the signature—not verifying the information, but simply witnessing the signature. Sometimes laws are made funny. The two men sign in as Guests, then as Verifiers, nod goodbye, and wade into the partying crowds.

Powder blue notices some of the men and women are dressed to the nines, others look like they've outfitted themselves at the Salvation Army. They mix together, though, and hover over traditional craps tables and roulette wheels, placing their bets. Others sit with fanned-out playing cards in front of them, trying to look calm, cool, pensive.

In an area like a living room, a dozen cheering people sit on edges of their chairs and couches clutching paper tickets while on the big-screen TV the small crouching riders press themselves tight against the necks of straining horses.

At tables, women and men, some barely out of high school, many well into retirement, sip drinks and inhale smoke from cigarettes. They pause from time to time to grip coins with thumb and forefinger and scratch silver spots from tiny cards.

The man in the powder blue suit takes it all in.

There are variations on old themes, too, he notices. A half dozen women and men dance in a circle around six folding chairs. Powder blue recognizes one of the women as a former gymnast and ballet dancer who had been a scholar-athlete in high school and college. She is both smart and agile, a combination she is no doubt counting on to help her at Casino Night. A husky man—who looks like he could swap jackets with a waiter and fit in, which he could, since he's with the House—holds a boom box that plays an inane Jack-in-the-Box tune over and over. He steps into the circle of chair dancers and removes one of the six folding chairs.

Nearby two men sit facing one another over a board game—something like chess—both concentrating intently. A third man, obviously House, sits along the sideline of the table, like a line judge at a tennis match. He holds an old-fashioned stopwatch and periodically gives the men updates on time remaining. One of the two Guests smokes incessantly, the other licks his lips nervously as if wishing he had a cigarette, too. Both take frequent hefty swigs of their free drinks, which the cocktail waiters replenish at a snap of the House timekeeper's fingers. The timekeeper himself doesn't smoke, drink, or make conversation; he simply looks impassive, making sure his face gives no look that might imply one Guest or the other has made a good or bad move.

The man in the powder blue suit notices a cordoned-off area, like a yellow-striped pedestrian crossing. The marked zone, however, is long and narrow, perhaps six feet wide and forty feet long, like the runway which track-and-field stars—long jumpers, broad jumpers, triple jumpers—might use.

He sees a crowd gathered around one of the gaming tables, and when he draws closer, he spots the man in the red turtleneck—the man who witnessed for him, the man he witnessed for—using his forearms to corral his plastic chips into a tight pile. The House attendant waits patiently while the man in the turtleneck herds all of the chips onto Number Eight and picks up the dice. He's betting the farm.

Powder blue creeps closer, but it's not curiosity—

it's envy. He can almost feel himself shaking the spotted bones, can hear their rattle in his ears, can practically smell them in his own sweaty, oily hands.

But then he's aware, quite suddenly, violently, of the inane Jack-in-the-Box music—not because he hears it, but because he stops hearing it. It ceases in mid-tune. He snaps around toward the circle of chair dancers. The six scramble for seats—musical chairs for adventurous adults, what will they think of next?—but the scholar-athlete loses her balance as a sweaty fat man leans a meaty forearm into the small of her back. Plop! She misses the folding chair and lands heavily, unceremoniously, on the floor. The fat man claims the seat, and the other four have seats as well. As the woman on the floor begins to weep, the House attendant restarts the Jack-in-the-Box tune and urges the five seated Guests to their feet again while he removes another chair, leaving four. A too kind waitress sets aside a platter of hors d'oeuvres and calms the scholar-athlete as she leads her away.

The man in powder blue shakes his head—tough break, nice lady—then turns back to look for the red turtleneck whose pile of chips has tripled. He bets it all on Eight again, and the dice explode out of his hand, bouncing and clattering the length of the green felt-covered table. They come to rest. Seven. The crowd groans. A moment of reverent silence follows. Grief. Then the applause starts, and soon the entire roof resounds with clapping and hooting for this fellow in the red turtleneck who has just lost the farm. He bows to the crowd like a knight before a queen, acknowledging their ovation, and is led away from the table.

At the table for two the House line judge stands and watches the two Guests shaking hands over the board game. The smoker lights up a fresh one and collapses into his chair, exhausted. His humbled opponent, shoulders bowed, licks his lips and walks away as directed to join the others.

Not far off, a tower clock in a church steeple begins to bong in the night air. The man in the blue suit sees fifteen people lined up at the plush red velvet rope (everything so classy at Casino Night) that cordons off the yellow zone. One man licks his lips nervously, trying to shut out the sounds of the wailing woman on his arm who cries about children-at-home and why-did-he-do-it? The ballet dancer/gymnast with the bruised pride and derriere dabs at her puffy eyes with a handkerchief a House waiter has given her. The man in the red turtleneck stands resolutely with his hands clenched into fists in his pants pockets.

In the black night sky the Japanese lanterns burn bright. The other Guests gather in silence to watch the fifteen, thinking perhaps: There, but for the grace of God, go I.

The tower clock strikes six on its way to eight and a House usher—just like at the theater—unclips the red velvet cordon rope and draws it aside. No tickets to take here, though.

The clock strikes seven, and the fifteen line up by threes, clasping hands. Five straight rows. And as the clock strikes Eight (turtleneck had said an Eight was to die for) the first trio lurches forward, racing along the runway, gathering speed like Olympic jumpers—then the second trio right behind, and the third and fourth and fifth, some screaming, some crying, some silent—until they hurtle out onto the empty night air, their voices echoing in the canyons between buildings.

Directly below, a minister, a priest, and a rabbi are standing in a parking lot, standing as if in some weird prayer circle and holding onto what looks like a giant hula hoop that's got something like a skin stretched tightly across it. They're swaying from side to side, here and there, like drunken sailors, eyes lifted heavenward. They hear the clock strike Eight and steady themselves to catch whoever they can. If they'd only come one at a time, there might be a chance. (There used to be six on the ring, but the social worker was transferred and the Buddhist and the nun were killed by falling gamblers.) But even with three, they try. They try, but they keep tripping over bodies from the seven o'clock jump and the underlayer from the six o'clock jump. They try, the minister, the priest, and the rabbi.

And to the man in the powder blue suit peering down from Casino Night, the three look like circus clowns who have arrived to climb out of a miniature firetruck. Yes, they're firefighter clowns, maneuvering back and forth with only their hope and naive courage, trying to respond to a horrendous rooftop clown fire. Powder blue shakes his head.

The Guests return to what they were doing. Six new Guests wait at the lectern, witnessing one another in. On the back of the lectern, where he hadn't noticed it before, is a small sign—the hot-line number for Gamblers Anonymous. Powder blue looks pensive. He could call them, or call his G.A. sponsor, his buddy. But, though his palms are sweaty and the dice are calling to him, he has so far tonight been able to resist. But then again, what's left to lose? The house is gone, and the bank accounts, and the family. Nothing's left but the clothes on his back and the car. He glances again at the hot-line number, then back down at the three clowns ten stories down in the parking lot. He knows what he has to do. He makes a megaphone with his hands, hushes the crowd.

"Great odds," he says. "Cover me at five to one." He holds up his registration in one hand and jingles his car keys in the other. "Five to one against my $50,000 Porsche. My $50,000 Porsche says if I jump with the nine o'clock group, the guys with the net—*if they catch anybody*—will catch me. I'm looking for five to one. Five to one, anybody?"

Hands, many hands, go up, and powder blue feels alive again.

The Witness Tree

"The Witness Tree" is at its heart a mystery story. More accurately, it is a story about a mystery, the mystery of evil. It appeared in *Shadows and Silence* (December 2000), the acclaimed hardcover anthology from World Fantasy Award-winning and Bram Stoker Award-winning Ash-Tree Press. It was named Honorable Mention in *Year's Best Fantasy & Horror #14*, 2001.

When the monstrous tower bell at Old South Church started humming of its own accord the week before Halloween, Dutch Roberts, the town constable for Norwich, Vermont, called me and Devaney to check it out. He didn't call us to evaluate the bell, not in the operational or scientific sense—we're not structural engineers. And he didn't call us to investigate it—we're not ghost busters, either. He called us to get us to check out the story—we're reporters, plain old, garden-variety, small-town reporters for The Valley News, the daily serving the Upper Valley of the Connecticut River, which forms the border of western New Hampshire and eastern Vermont.

I say we're reporters. Actually, I'm the reporter. Devaney's my father-in-law, a retired high school history teacher who's an inveterate shutterbug. He shoots pictures to accompany my stories. Most of the shots are of fender-benders, or a nursing home resident turning a hundred, or a pig-tailed girl riding on her father's shoulders at a parade. Not that I couldn't shoot my own photos, which I did before Devaney became my side-kick, but he's decent company, and working part-time as a stringer photographer keeps him out of my moth-er-in-law's hair.

So when the two hundred year-old tower bell start-ed humming, Dutch called me to ask if I wanted a Halloween story with a local angle.

The story swallowed a lot more time than anyone imagined it would.

The day after Dutch called, Devaney and I drove to Norwich to meet with him and Reverend Halliday, Old South's pastor. The four of us stood in front of the church, staring up at the steeple as Reverend Halliday recounted the story, Dutch filling in details here and there.

The bell had begun humming ten days earlier, on a Sunday night around the middle of the month. A handful of teenagers in the church's Youth Group had noticed it first, when they were playing hide-and-seek around the church and one of them had sneaked up into the belfry. The lad reported the deep hum to the Youth Group chaperones, who further reported it to the building sexton who, unable to find any source for the bell's vibration, consulted Reverend Halliday, who called in several of the Buildings and Grounds Committee. No one had an answer, only such theories as "mild, sustained earthquake" and "static electrici-ty." Eventually the tale of the mysterious humming bell got around to Dutch Roberts, who investigated and suggested the church call a structural engineer, which they did. The structural engineer uncovered nothing.

As we stood craning our necks to look up at the bell, I could faintly hear a sound deep and low, about the frequency of distant thunder. Except that it was a steady tone, like monks chanting a single mantra, an

Om, deeper even than the hum of a transformer on a light pole.

"Can we go up?" I asked as Devaney snapped a couple of 35mm shots from the sidewalk and across the road by the white board fence surrounding the village green.

"Be my guest," Reverend Halliday said. "Dutch can show you the way up. My asthma prevents my climbing that ladder."

"Some day you ought to come up, Reverend," Dutch said. "The view from there is *in-spire-ing.*" Dutch laughed at his own joke after he said it.

"I'll just have to imagine it, Dutch," the pastor said humorlessly, waving goodbye as he walked toward the manse next door. "Enjoy the view. Good to meet you gents."

Except for the low hum of the bell, we found nothing out of the ordinary. It was cast iron, made in Boston by the famous Colonial silversmith Paul Revere, and measured nearly five feet in diameter. It no longer swung and tilted to operate the clapper as it once had, but was now fixed and had a hammer that struck it on the hour to give the ringing sound. The hum we had heard from the sidewalk below wasn't much louder than it had seemed earlier—in fact, we could comfortably talk over it when we first climbed into the tower. Nor was it painful to our ears—at first. After awhile, though—I suppose because we were standing directly beside it—the steady vibration began to annoy my ears and then hurt them. It reminded me of my pup's annoyance whenever I hummed in his ear, how he'd tolerate it briefly, then give a twitch of his ear, and finally walk away from me.

"No kidding about this view," I said, scanning the town from my bird's perch. "This is an amazing vantage point. You can see everything."

"And look at the view of the green," Devaney said, focusing for a long-distance shot, then for a zoom. "Oh, imagine what this bell has seen in two hundred years. The stories it could tell."

"Parades and church fairs and carnivals and kite flying," I said.

"Kids making out on the green on warm summer nights," Devaney chimed in.

"More than making out," Dutch added. "I've had to throw cold water on 'em more than once."

The three of us laughed and turned back to the ladder. Our inspection had lasted less than five minutes. I noted that though the bell hummed, nothing vibrated, not the decking we stood on, not the stairs of the ladder, hardly even the bell when I *felt* it. Even though I was no engineer, I had passed my science classes and knew sound was produced by vibration, and if the bell was vibrating at all, there had to be a source. But neither I nor others who had checked earlier for a source could locate it.

Devaney and I thanked Dutch for the tour and told him we wanted to look around the village proper, perhaps interview a few locals about this strange phenomenon. He volunteered the names of the Youth Group teens in case we wanted to talk with them. So off we went on a walking tour of this quaint New England village.

We learned something right away, something which could easily have proven irrelevant. But because I was searching for something that might tie into a Halloween theme for a story, I took notes on even the seemingly unrelated.

Such as: The first things a visitor notices upon leaving Interstate Route 91 at Norwich, Vermont, are the neat, black-shuttered houses which are so quintessentially New England. Then comes the historic village green, which you look through, as through a camera's viewfinder, to see Old South Church fifty yards beyond the far side of the green. The white board fence around the green perfectly centers Old South for pictures, which explains why the church has graced more Christmas cards, calendars, and coffee table books than any other church in Vermont.

On the edge of the green, beside the roadside turnout where visitors park in order to take pictures, a large blue and gold plaque proclaims Norwich's downtown to be on the National Historic Register.

But under that plaque is yet another plaque, erected by the Friends of Norwich, which tells the story of the Norwich Witch.

In 1793, ten years after Norwich was granted its charter, and a hundred years after the Salem, Massachusetts witch trials, Hester Glynn, a young woman thrice widowed, was accused of being a witch. Her accuser was a seventy-five year-old minister, John Ogletree, not from Norwich but from across the Connecticut River at Hanover, New Hampshire, home to Dartmouth College.

Influenced by the stories of the Salem witch trials told him in his youth by his hellfire-and-brimstone minister/grandfather, Ogletree became convinced that the widow Glynn—"thrice widowed, so beware becoming her fourth," he cautioned—was responsible for a "veil of evil" which hung over the village. Ogletree actually preferred charges against Mrs. Glynn, but his accusations were laughed out of court.

Then one morning Widow Glynn's body was found at the back corner of the village green, beneath the spreading arms and heart-shaped leaves of a more-than-hundred year-old linden tree. Her throat had been slit, and dark blood soaked the ground around the linden tree's roots. The Reverend Ogletree was nowhere to be found, and rumors circulated quickly that he had fled the area. An arrest warrant was issued, but folks were certain he'd never show his face again, and there was no pursuit. So went the legend of the Norwich Witch.

After a bit of rummaging for information, Devaney and I learned that on July 4, 1976, to commemorate the nation's Bicentennial, the Friends of Norwich had planted a blue spruce on the back corner of the green, practically in the shadow of the roughly three hundred year-old linden tree where Widow Glynn's body had been discovered. I surmised that though the Friends of Norwich wanted to commemorate the Bicentennial, there was perhaps a dollop of superstition present, too—perhaps the notion of good cancelling out past evil? Devaney snapped a photo of the Friends of Norwich plaque, then took a zoom of the blue spruce with the huge, spreading linden behind it. The tree was known far and wide for its heart-shaped leaves.

"Shame about the grass," said Devaney, putting away his camera. I nodded my head. Both trees—the linden and the spruce—were healthy and flourishing, but around the base of the linden was a rough, barren patch spreading some twenty-five feet from the tree in every direction. "Looks like they could do with some fertilizer."

Mrs. Corcoran at the Town Hall advanced the story of the blue spruce for us, explaining that from the 1976 planting grew not only a tree but a tradition—the decorating of the blue spruce, the Norwich Christmas Tree, on the first Sunday in December. Then, a couple of weeks after the decorating, on the Sunday evening before Christmas, the townfolk and visitors would gather around it to sing *O Christmas Tree*. Afterward everyone would cross the green to Old South Church, gather in front of the outdoor manger scene, sing *O*

Little Town of Bethlehem and *Silent Night*, and go inside for hot chocolate and mulled cider. It had become a tradition which young and old alike looked forward to. Devaney took a picture of a smiling Mrs. Corcoran sitting at her desk with the phone to her ear.

The next day we interviewed the Youth Group kids after school. Their theory about the humming tower bell was that it was receiving a signal from space, either from a far-off galaxy or maybe from something closer, like a satellite.

"After all," one of them said, "if your teeth can pick up radio stations in the fillings . . ."

Devaney got the kids to pose on the manse steps for a group portrait.

The newspaper published my local-interest story and Devaney's photos in the edition which appeared two days before Halloween. Because it was still basically a story about an unexplainable humming bell, with no scientific testing or analysis to report, I related it in a straightforward manner. There just didn't seem to be a way to get a spooky angle on it. We figured the paper would sell well in Norwich because of all the photos of local folks, making for paste-ins for family scrapbooks, that sort of thing. I figured that was the end of it.

On All Saints' Day, November first, the morning after Halloween, Dutch Roberts phoned me at home. "Six reports of missing dogs last night," he said into the phone. He sounded to me like he was trying to keep his voice even.

"Six?" I said. "Dognappers? Halloween prank?" I let the question hang in the air.

"Dammit, Hoagie," Dutch said. "This is serious."

I apologized for sounding flip.

"The six dogs all belonged to families who live within a block of Old South," he said.

"I take it the dogs weren't on leashes?" I said.

"People in Florida have been known to lose pets right off the leash. Alligators, you know."

"Hoag!" Dutch said, squeezing his voice so that a yell came out at an almost normal tone.

"Okay," I said. "I'll get Devaney and we'll be right down."

A half hour later we walked into Dutch Roberts's constable's office. About fifteen people sat or stood there. Their squabbling dissipated when we stepped in. Even though it was November, the small office was warm and muggy from so many people breathing and talking in it.

I wanted to ask Dutch, "So why'd you call me?" But I held my tongue.

"So, folks, please," Dutch said. "I know you're upset, but try to remain calm. I've notified the Vermont and New Hampshire State Police. They'll be on the lookout. And we'll put out the word around town to keep an eye out for your pets. If you have pictures of your dogs, please bring them by sometime today."

Then, nodding toward me and Devaney, "I'm sure Mr. Hoag here will help in any way he can by doing a newspaper story on this situation." Several people started to talk at the same time, but Dutch stopped them by saying, "Please, friends, could you excuse us for a few minutes? I've got to meet with Mr. Hoag and Mr. Devaney. You can talk with him after that." He gently shooed them from his office, closed the door, and invited me and Devaney to sit. Dutch closed his eyes, made a steeple with his fingers, and hooked his thumbs under his chin. He let out a tired sigh.

"They're scared some Satanic cult sacrificed their animals last night," he said. "In a Halloween ritual." He opened his eyes and caught my questioning look. "I assured them there have been no reports of cults operating in this area," he said.

The three of us sat silent for a moment. Dutch scratched his head.

"Think it's local kids, neighborhood kids?" Devaney volunteered. "Their own kids, maybe?"

Dutch shook his head. "Nah. Most of the kids were home and in bed already. The younger ones had done their trick-or-treating and the older ones were finished hell-raising. No, as was usual for these dogs, they were all let out to pee after nine o'clock. Five of them go out and do their duty on their own, then return after five or ten minutes. One gets walked by his master near the church."

"And?" Devaney asked. "Did the person see where his dog went, or what happened to it?"

I could see the veins in Dutch's temples throbbing. "As a matter of fact, the man saw his dog wandering along the fence next to the green. But he says when he turned to look up at the tower clock, the dog disappeared. He whistled and called and searched for it for an hour and a half."

"So the dog disappeared right on the hour?" I asked.

"No, fellow said it was around ten-fifteen or ten-thirty," Dutch said.

"So why'd he look up at the clock?" Devaney interrupted. "It wasn't striking the hour. What got his attention?"

Dutch looked blankly at us, then picked up the phone. He dialed a number scrawled on his desk pad.

"Ronald? Yeah. This is Dutch at the constable's office. I forgot to ask you—what made you look up at the tower clock when you did?"

Devaney and I looked at each other, shrugged our shoulders and made faces that mockingly said this was a story for *The Twilight Zone*.

"Didn't hear or see anything else, then?" Dutch

continued. "Just the hum getting louder?" A few more nods of the head and Dutch said, "Call if you think of anything else," then hung up.

Our faces must have said, "Well?"

"Ronald Trask. He says when the dog walked away from him to go do its duty, the hum of the bell increased in intensity a notch."

"You mean it went up a decibel? Got louder? What was he saying?" I pressed.

"Those are Ronald's words. 'It increased in intensity a notch.' He said it wasn't the same as getting louder, but it was more intense, more urgent."

"More *urgent?* Those his words, too?" I asked. "More *urgent*? For Chrissakes, Dutch. It's a bell, a stupid frigging bell!"

"Calm down, Hoagie," Devaney said, placing a hand on my wrist. "Let Dutch tell it. Whaddya say, Dutch?"

"The guy just lost his dog. In looking back on what happened, he believes the bell was trying to tell him something," Dutch said.

"Like *warn* him?" I asked impatiently.

"Look, Hoag," Dutch said. "You can interview the guy if you want to. Hell, you can talk to the other dog owners who lost dogs last night, too. You can interview everybody who's got a dog, cat, or parakeet if you want to. Go ahead. You have my blessing."

The three of us sat a couple of minutes, Dutch and me trying to cool down. We weren't mad at each other. We simply had a mystery that was frustrating us both.

"If it was a Satanic thing," Devaney said, "you know, a sacrifice, don't you think they'd have just used one dog? My money's on dognappers. I heard they grab healthy animals and sell 'em to laboratories for experimentation. Halloween night'd be a perfect time. It's a great cover."

Rather than mire ourselves in further discussion and conjecture, we seemed to agree by either consensus or default that Devaney's dognapping theory carried the most weight for the time being. We left Dutch in his office chair and I went home and typed up the missing dogs story, which was simply a short news item.

The following Friday Dutch called me again. Curt Chase, the custodian at the Elementary School which bordered the green, reported to the constable's office that the earth beneath the linden tree at Witch's Corner, close to the blue spruce, had become even more bare than before. The radius of barren ground had widened to thirty-five feet from the tree's base. Sure enough, when Devaney checked the shot he'd taken from the green and compared the bare ground in his photo to the bare ground Curt Chase reported, it had grown ten feet in its radius. Something was killing the grass, Curt Chase noted, but he also commented that neither the linden nor the blue spruce seemed adversely affected.

"In fact," Curt said when Devaney and I caught up to him for a quick interview outside the school, "the trees appear healthier than ever, the way a houseplant perks up and shines after you give it some plant food."

Devaney took a couple of close-ups of the two trees at Witch's Corner. When he developed the film later in the day, he compared them to the telephoto shots he had taken of the trees the day we had read the Friends of Norwich plaque. Although we couldn't be absolutely certain, the trees did indeed seem to look healthier, which was strange because the peak of Vermont's colorful foliage season had passed nearly a month earlier, so the linden's leaves should have been shrinking back, not expanding.

The next day Dutch called and said he had a dozen

reports of cats missing, plus two more dogs, several chickens and roosters, and a Vietnamese pot-bellied pig. These I gave more space than a news item—this was Page Three stuff—relating the past Norwich animal disappearances as well. I also interviewed people on the street in Norwich, finding that many people believed the hum of the bell had grown either louder or more intense—but that was a separate news item.

Meanwhile Devaney and I pored over the church records, town records, and the public library's historic documents, all in search of any background information we might use in future articles. Whenever we found a page or paragraph we thought would prove helpful later, Devaney photographed it. We became fairly adept at deciphering the cursive script of our seventeenth, eighteenth, and nineteenth century ancestors.

Over the Thanksgiving weekend, when my wife Carol and I were at her parents' house for the traditional roast turkey dinner, the family got to looking at old photo albums. After an hour or so we worked up to more current pictures that Devaney had taken—the new roof we'd put on his garage, Carol and her mother on a porch swing together, a colorful shot of the changing leaves on the tree behind the house.

"Oops," Devaney said. "The rest of these are from last month's Norwich trip, Hoagie, when we went with Dutch Roberts up into the bell tower at Old South. I had a couple of exposures left on that family roll."

We fanned the pictures across the dining room table. Dutch and me with the bell behind us. A distant shot of the green taken from the steeple.

"Hey, what's that?" Devaney said, pointing to a zoom shot of the green.

We both looked closer. "What is *what*?" I said.

"There," Devaney said. "By that huge tree, the

linden, in the Witch's Corner. Looks like a rope coming from the base of it."

I examined the picture again.

"Looks like a dead groundhog or a possum out at the end of it," I said. "Like the rope's around its neck."

"So the other end's tied to the tree?" Devaney asked, looking puzzled.

"Can't tell," I said. "Your picture doesn't quite show it. You're shooting downward and these branches obscure the base of the trunk."

"Maybe there's somebody behind the tree, holding the rope," Carol offered.

"Kids?" my mother-in-law said.

The four of us sat pondering a minute.

"No," I said thoughtfully. "The kids were in school when we were there. Besides, it looks to me more like the rope goes right to the tree, not behind it."

"Maybe some kids tied the animal to the tree during recess or lunch," my mother-in-law said. "Or maybe it's a pet, a dog that looks like a groundhog. Maybe they came back for it later."

"That's a mighty thick rope," Carol said. "Hairy, I'd say."

Devaney pointed to the photos he had taken after we descended the bell tower, the ones by the Friends of Norwich plaque. The blue spruce and the towering linden tree were prominent in the background.

"Look here," he said. "I took these pictures not long after the tower shots. Look at the green in the background, and the trees. There's no rope in these pictures. And no groundhog."

"So you're saying that these kids removed the animal and the rope while you were climbing down from the church tower?" my mother-in-law asked.

"Ma," Carol said impatiently. "Nobody said it was kids."

I put my hand up, symbolically stepping between mother and daughter.

"I don't know *what* we're saying," I said, "except that this rope and animal aren't tied to the tree in the later pictures."

The next day we looked at the photos with Dutch Roberts. He concluded that our rope looked more like a thick vine, the kind we had swung on as kids, the ones which snaked up into trees in swampy areas. He was certain the animal was a groundhog, though he referred to it as a woodchuck. He refused to revisit Devaney's Satanic-cult/animal-sacrifice theory, though he wasn't about to dismiss it either.

"It'd be too hard to catch a wild woodchuck," he said. "And why bother if you've got access to tame pets?"

On the first Sunday in December, with the help of the Highway Department's backhoe tractor, the Friends of Norwich decorated the Norwich Christmas Tree as usual. They hung colored lights all over the blue spruce and attached foil-wrapped gift boxes to its branches. Although there was no story for me to write, Devaney wanted to shoot pictures of the tree-trimming, so he talked me into accompanying him for a change.

Later that same day the Old South Youth Group set up the manger scene in front of the church. The kids remembered Devaney and me, and rewarded him with schleppy poses for pictures.

During both events, the tree-trimming party and the manger scene set-up, the tower bell hummed the way a dog growls at a stranger. And for the first time I understood what people had been describing. I *felt* it. The intensity, the growing urgency, the warning.

A stray cat living under Marciano's Italian Ristorante disappeared that night. I wouldn't have known except that Marciano himself called two nights later to tell me, knowing I had been on top of the pet-nappings. Everyone in town was tuned in to it. Marciano didn't really notice the cat was *gone*, he simply observed that over the next few days the scraps he put out weren't being eaten. This from a cat that had eaten at Marciano's rear door every night for two years.

Oddly enough, no roadkill carcasses were reported on any of the Norwich streets—no skunks, no possums, no raccoons, no cats. In a normal autumn the town's animal control officer or the Highway Department would get two or three cleanup calls a week.

The Sunday before Christmas arrived, and with it came Caroling Eve, which Devaney and I decided we'd attend. By four o'clock, with daylight fading, the caroling began, as always, at the Witch's Corner with *O Christmas Tree.* Another carol followed. Just as it got dark, someone threw a switch and the strings of colored lights blinked on. Everyone, especially those with toddlers, oohed and aahed. Then the crowd meandered across the green toward Old South's manger scene, singing as they strolled. Devaney and I lagged behind so he could snap a few pictures of the Christmas tree.

About that time Jim and Tanya Hathaway, one of the couples we had interviewed when their Doberman disappeared, missed signals on who was watching Joshua, their three year-old. Jim had Eric, and Tanya had Etta. Each assumed the other had Josh. From where Devaney and I were standing, we could see what happened.

Josh's attention span for the tree-lighting ceremony had been short. He'd discovered a great place to push his little dump truck around, under the huge three hundred year-old linden tree. His playground was a bare patch of ground as calloused as an oiled Vermont dirt road. The truck wheels moved so freely, and the tree lights made it so easy to see. Devaney and I had been so caught up in the picture-taking that we had failed to notice him at first.

Josh had gotten deeply involved in his play and failed to notice that the singers, including his parents, had drifted across the green toward Old South, whose humming tower bell grew steadily more urgent. It drew my attention the way Ronald Trask said it drew his on Halloween night, when he lost his dog while walking it. I could feel the bell growling a warning.

As Devaney snapped pictures of the Christmas tree, I glanced over at little Josh playing innocently with his dump truck under the linden tree. That's when I saw the movement he didn't see—the root, brushing, swishing, sweeping. I not only saw it—I was certain I *heard* it, too, even over the rising hum of the bell. It swished softly like a tail, deceptively caressing the ground the way a feather duster brushes the surface of a table, the root all the while slithering toward the unknowing boy.

"Josh!" I heard, but it wasn't my voice. It was his mother's scream, and for a moment my gaze left the boy as I turned my head to look toward Tanya Hathaway as she raced across the green. Her husband Jim and their two other children stood by the manger scene in front of the church, looking confused as she ran from them.

The bell above started to tremble and rumble. From a hundred yards away I could hear it throbbing. Then the ground under our feet began to shake, and I heard someone near the church yell, "Earthquake!" People dropped to the ground.

"The kid!" It was Devaney's voice behind me. "Hoagie, get the kid!"

"Josh!" Tanya Hathaway screamed as she raced for him. "Josh!"

The root swished side to side, closing within five feet of the child. I had no idea if it had lightning speed and struck like a cobra or if it slowly strangled its victims like a boa constrictor. Maybe it could do either. It could surely have its way with this prey, a clumsy three year-old.

As I started toward him, Josh heard his mother's screams and looked up, realizing for the first time that he was alone. He clapped his hands to his ears, not to shut out his mother's voice, but to escape the deafening din of the bell, which sounded like a boiler about to explode now. As it crescendoed, I could make out dogs howling all over town as if a fire siren had sounded.

I think Devaney's flash went off behind me then, because I caught a momentary glimpse of the base of the linden tree. In that bright moment, I swear, I could clearly see the whip-root emerging directly from the tree's trunk at ground level. In that split second I was reminded of the rabbit hole, the White Rabbit, and Alice.

The root coiled itself near the child now, like a rattlesnake.

"Josh!" Tanya screamed, she and I each six feet from the boy. The boy held out his arms to her, and I held up the only thing I had—my spiral reporter's notebook—between the child and the ready-to-strike snake-root.

Crack! A line of electricity—pure energy, Devaney later told me, arced from the sky to the church bell then—not soft summer heat-lightning, but a vivid, violent, terrible-swift-sword sort of lightning, thunder-cracking lightning, the lightning of judgment—sizzling as it shot forth from the heavens. It refracted off the bell, never touching the square steeple that housed it, crackled high above the green, and grounded itself in the rabbit hole, the open throat of the linden trunk.

Kaboom! The tree exploded, shooting out of the ground like a rocket at Cape Canaveral, trunk clearing the ground, roots trailing like a nest of angry snakes. The tree disintegrated in mid-air, shattered into a million tiny fragments. A blood-curdling scream filled the air as it blew apart.

The blast threw Josh, his mother, and me twenty feet out onto the center of the green. When I sat up, I saw Tanya lying near me, crying hysterically and clutching her babbling child. Soot rained everywhere like volcanic ash. Foil-covered gift boxes, blown off the adjacent blue spruce, lay scattered all around us.

"Holy maracas!" I heard Devaney say. "Talk about fireworks!" When I looked to where his voice had come from, I saw him lying on his side near the white board fence, camera beside him.

The crowd from the manger, including Jim Hathaway and his two other children, made its way across the green to Tanya, Josh, Devaney, and me. Dutch and the others stood staring at the crater where the linden tree had stood. The hole was seven feet deep and fifteen or twenty feet across the center. All around the green were splinters and small pieces of the tree, though no single piece was longer than two feet. The lightning strike had practically pulverized it.

"Hey, look down there!" someone yelled. "In the hole!"

While Jim Hathaway and several others comforted Tanya and Josh, a group of us peered into the crater. Flashlights shone on someone in the crater, crouched in the center.

"What the—?" Dutch said. "Who is it?"

No one answered. The figure, as far as we could

see, was clad in a black suit and black hat. I didn't recall anyone reported missing.

"My Rusty!" Ronald Trask yelped, pointing down into the crater. There beside the person lay the carcass of a dog, its neck wrapped in a hairy root.

Rusty wasn't the only lost pet in the crater. We made out the carcasses of dozens of dogs, cats, and other animals in various states of decomposition, each with a root strangling it, the roots all leading back to the body.

Nobody, not even Dutch Roberts, the constable, wanted to jump down into the pit, which was beginning to stink of rotting flesh. Finally Devaney stepped past me and, before I could stop him, jumped in, camera in hand.

"Shine those lights on his face," Devaney ordered, pointing to the black-suited man who appeared to be sitting. Devaney lined up for a shot.

"Who is it?" I called down. The odor drifting up from the crater was beginning to turn my stomach.

"Can't tell," Devaney said. "It's mostly hair and clothes on a skeleton. Long gone. Looks like his hands were tied by the tree roots."

"And what about all those other roots?" Dutch said. "The ones wrapped around the animals?"

Devaney examined the scene more closely.

"Geez," he said. "Those roots all lead back to the skeleton's mouth."

"To its mouth?" I asked. "Not its hands?"

"Looks like it," he answered. "To the mouth. Throw me a flashlight and I'll make sure."

Dutch tossed one down into the hole, but Devaney missed catching it. The heavy flashlight bounced off his hand and struck the root that had strangled the pot-bellied pig.

"Cripes," Devaney said. "That gashed the root. It's

oozing." He bent over and retrieved the flashlight, shining it on the damaged root.

"Well?" Dutch asked.

"Looks like blood," Devaney said.

The foul odor wafting up out of the hole was getting to me, and though I wanted to jump in to get the story, I couldn't. I pinched my nostrils and breathed through my mouth.

"Move over, Devaney," Dutch yelled. "I'm coming down."

In a second Dutch was in the hole, standing beside Devaney. He prodded the root near the gash, then pressed the sole of his boot down on the root between the potbellied pig and the gash. The root oozed a little more.

"It's like a transfusion or something, I think," Devaney said.

"See if the root taps into the pig's skin," I called down.

Devaney pulled a pair of gloves out of his coat pocket and put them on. Dutch, not having gloves, pulled a handkerchief from his back pocket and wrapped it around one hand. Together they grabbed the part of the root coiled around the pig's neck.

"Ooh, geezum," Devaney said, making a face of disgust. "It's squishy, like a—"

"*Tongue*," Dutch finished for him as they both pulled their hands back. "It's like grabbing a tongue."

"Yeah," Devaney agreed.

"Okay, okay," I said. "So it feels like a tongue. Does it break the pig's skin?"

Devaney stripped off his gloves and handed them to Dutch.

"You check it," he said to the constable. "I'll shoot the pictures." His fingers returned to something they felt more comfortable with, his camera.

Dutch unwound whatever it was that had wrapped itself around the small pig's throat. He shined the light close around the dead animal's neck.

"No," Dutch said. "It was just coiled around. Maybe strangled it. But no broken skin that I can see."

Devaney snapped a couple of shots.

"Now the other end," I said in my nasally voice.

"The ass?" Dutch said, looking up at me with genuine puzzlement on his face.

"Not the other end of the pig," I said impatiently. "The other end of the root."

I heard Devaney chuckle. Down there in the midst of that carnage and stench, he was able to chuckle.

"Oh," Dutch said, swinging the beam of his flashlight around toward the black-suited skeleton. I watched the light move from the restrained wrists to the skull's mouth.

"This is weird," Dutch said.

"What is?" I asked.

Devaney and Dutch looked at each other, and Devaney said, "It could actually be a tongue, Hoagie."

"What do you mean, a tongue?" I said.

"A tongue," Dutch answered. "It looks like every one of the roots that are wrapped around these animals are coming out of this skeleton's mouth."

"Then what's holding the skeleton's wrists?" Devaney said, continuing to click away with his camera.

"The *tree's* roots," Dutch said, touching the wrist restraints with his gloved hands. "These are live roots, tough ones. Different from the squishy stuff that came out of Mr. What's-his-name's mouth. They looked the same in the dark, at least they did from a distance, but they're definitely different. Tree roots holding the skeleton's wrists, and the skeleton's tongue holding the dead animals."

While I stood there pondering what it might mean,

I noticed that everyone else had withdrawn, probably because of the stench. I had no idea how long there had been only the three of us there alone. I also noticed that two police cars and several firetrucks were screeching up in front of the church. At least the tower bell had stopped its humming.

"Cops and fire department are here, guys," I said down into the hole. "They're coming across the green. Do a quick check and see if there's any I.D. on the skeleton."

Dutch took off one glove and patted down the loose-hanging suit.

"No pockets in these old trousers," he said. "No zipper, either. And no side pockets or vest pockets in the suit coat," he said.

"The hat?" I heard Devaney ask, and saw Dutch lift it. A sheet of paper fluttered from under it.

"What's it say?" I asked. "Hurry! They're coming."

"I can't read it," Dutch said. "It's that old kind of writing. Like in George Washington's time."

"Give it here," Devaney said sharply. "I can read that stuff pretty well now." He glanced over it. "It says: *I have decided to tell the truth.*"

"But it's not signed," Dutch said.

That's when the police and firefighters descended upon the scene of destruction. They helped Dutch and Devaney out of the crater, then took statements from the three of us, along with everyone else who had been around that night. Thank God they moved us into the manse for the interviews, getting us free of the stench of rotting animal carcasses. And thank God for small-town police work, because no one ever thought to ask Devaney for his camera or the rolls of film he shot that night.

I worked all night on the story while Devaney developed the film in his darkroom, so we had one heck of a scoop for the wire services the next morning. I wrote it as straight as I could, just reporting, not concluding anything. Other papers sent reporters who picked up the story after the fact, but they either headlined it "Norwich Christmas Miracle," emphasizing the disaster element and the fact that no one had been injured, or "Steeple Smites Christmas Tree," pitting the church and Christmas's true meaning over against the commercialism symbolized by the Christmas tree (even though the bolt of electricity had destroyed the linden tree while missing the blue spruce, liberating only its foil-wrapped boxes). All the stories listed "rare winter lightning" or "static electricity" as the cause.

Since there was no injury, loss of human life, or crime against a person committed (only against pets)—it being fairly clear that the skeleton was very, very old—the police sealed off the scene around the crater, but opted to wait until daylight to bring in the State Police investigators. The hole in the ground, the skeleton in the chair, and the rotting, stinking animal carcasses could wait six or eight hours.

The next day the investigators found "no tongue-like root wrapped around any animals, as bystanders claimed they saw the night before." They only found the dead animals. They did, however, find "the skeleton's wrists bound by the roots of the linden tree, which must have encircled the ulna and radius bones over a period of years." They also "located no scrap of old paper, which Mr. Roberts and Mr. Devaney claimed to have seen and which Mr. Devaney claimed to have read."

Unfortunately, Devaney had neglected to take a photo of the scrap of paper. The pictures from the crater—of the carcasses and the skeleton in the chair—showed what could have been a vine, a root, or even a rope, wrapped around the animals' necks and protruding from the skeleton's mouth, though whatever showed in the photos had miraculously evaporated by the next morning when investigators checked the crater. When we showed the shots to the police later, since their investigators had found no tongue-roots in the crater the morning after, they said they feared a hoax and would say so if we made the photos public.

The official report offered no conclusion, nor would the authorities speculate as to how the skeleton, a male's—estimated to be from around 1800—got under the main trunk of the tree. One interesting side note: the linden tree's age was estimated by a Forest Service expert to be three hundred fifty-four years old.

"Look, Hoagie," Devaney said to me a month later, after the police closed the books on the case. "We saw the lightning ricochet off the bell and splinter that tree, didn't we?"

I nodded my head.

"And I know what me and Dutch saw down in that hole," he continued.

"I'm with you, Devaney," I said, continuing to nod agreement. "Even from up on the green I'm pretty sure I saw something wrapped around those animals. And I think it led to our friend, the skeleton's, mouth."

We'd been over the story a hundred times.

"And Dutch saw the note under the hat, too," Devaney said.

"Yup," I agreed.

"And I know what I read."

We sat silent a moment.

"So what's your theory?" I asked.

"Probably same as yours," Devaney said.

"You think the bones are old Reverend Ogletree's, don't you?" I asked. "From 1793."

"Yup," Devaney said. "He's the one who slit Hester Glynn's throat. Agree?"

"I agree," I said. "They were having an affair and she threatened to expose it and ruin his reputation, or maybe he was having an affair and she found out and threatened to tell about it. Something along those lines."

"So he killed her at night," Devaney said.

"On the back corner of the green," I added.

"And then what?" Devaney said. "You think a small group of townspeople took the vigilante route, grabbed Ogletree, and planted the tree on top of him to mark the spot?"

"That theory wouldn't be bad," I said, "except that the linden tree wasn't *two* hundred years old years old, Devaney. Remember? The forester said it was *three* hundred fifty-four years old. So that tree was already a hundred and fifty-plus years old and extremely well-rooted when Hester Glynn was murdered in 1793. It must have been fairly formidable even then."

Devaney looked totally puzzled.

"So you're saying the townspeople didn't bury Ogletree and plant or move the tree on top of the site?" Devaney said.

"Correct," I said. "Besides, even if it were a handful of vigilantes, or even the whole town and they agreed to keep silent, why would they go to all that trouble to bury the murderer *under* the tree?"

Poor Devaney's face was a question mark.

"But you do agree the skeleton is old Ogletree, right?" he said. "And that Ogletree killed Hester Glynn because she threatened to expose him for some reason, whether it was an affair or something else?"

"Yes, to both questions," I said. "I think that mystery's solved."

"Then who buried him under the tree?" Devaney asked in frustration.

"*The tree*," I said, thinking of the heart-shaped leaves.

Devaney simply stared open-mouthed at me.

"I know this sounds crazy, but it's all I can figure. No one saw the horrific murder there on the back corner of the green *except the tree.* The tree was the only witness, and it knew there would be no justice, so *the tree dragged Ogletree down and held him."*

"Which explains the roots binding his wrists," Devaney said. "But what about all those dead animals? Dragged down by the tree, too? Why would it do that—to feed Ogletree?"

"No," I said. *"Ogletree dragged them down*—to sort of feed himself, although I don't think he was alive in the human way, living and breathing. I think all that was left was the evil, or the insanity, his essence. And that's what the tree had to hold captive for two hundred years. But, like the Bible says, no one has ever been able to tame the tongue. The tree could only restrain his hands and feet. The problem was, the evil was growing stronger again and Ogletree kept dragging more live bodies—animals—down beneath the tree. First it was small animals, then pets and larger animals—"

"And then," Devaney interrupted, "it went after a small person, little Josh Hathaway."

"Correct," I said.

"Which is why the lightning struck," Devaney said, even more animated now that more pieces of the puzzle were fitting together for him. "The bell began humming as the evil grew stronger, the way a dog growls, a sort of warning. And when Ogletree went for the kid, the church bell directed a lightning bolt at Ogletree."

"Yes, I think so," I said. "Either that or the lightning bolt used the bell. In any case, it appears the lightning and the bell coordinated their efforts."

"And zapped Ogletree," Devaney said.

"Exposed Ogletree," I said. "Or exposed the evil, at

least, and put a stop to the stalking. But I doubt the evil is destroyed. It never is."

"Like that Bible story," Devaney said. "About the evil spirits Jesus cast out of a man. He didn't destroy them. He sent them into a herd of pigs. But better in the pigs than in the man, I suppose."

"But Devaney," I asked. "Remember what happened to the pigs?"

"They went nuts and committed suicide. Stampeded off a cliff into the sea," he said.

"So where'd the evil spirits go after the pigs drowned?" I asked.

Devaney was stumped. "I don't know," he said. "Into the fish?"

I simply shrugged my shoulders. Where had the evil in Ogletree gone? Where does evil escape to, and where does it reside while it seeks a new host?

Perhaps there is no answer to that. Perhaps the best we can do is to pray. Pray for more linden trees. And preserve the ones we have.

Captain James's Bones

"Captain James's Bones," a campfire tale for pre-teens, is clearly in the Goosebumps vein. It first appeared as "Pemaquid Bone Yard Halloween" in *Lincoln County Weekly* (Damariscotta, Maine) on Halloween 1998 and was a read-aloud hit in coastal schools. The current version came out in a themed issue (ghost stories for/with children) of *All Hallows* (The Ghost Story Society, Canada) in October 2000.

I never play practical jokes any more, not since that night in the graveyard with the old captain's bones. Even today I feel somehow responsible for what happened.

It started when we moved to New Harbor as the school year began. My brother Willy started seventh grade, I started sixth. Fitting in at a new school was hard. Kids picked on me because I was small for my age, so Willy felt he had to defend me, which didn't win either of us any friends. We desperately wanted to fit in.

The week before Halloween we were sitting at lunch when Danny Gamage, an eighth-grader, started talking about the ghost of Captain James, who had perished in a shipwreck nearby at Pemaquid Point.

Willy's and my ears pricked up. All the other kids knew the story, but upon hearing Danny tell it again, their eyes grew wide. The story of the shipwreck was one locals knew by heart. In fact, it had been one of the first stories we heard when we moved to town.

Captain James's sailing ship had foundered on the rocks off Pemaquid Lighthouse one stormy night, and his crew and family had drowned. People on shore tried to rescue the captain but couldn't get to him. Pinned to the rocks in his yellow rain gear and yellow Sou'wester foul-weather hat, the waves dashed him to bits. His body was never recovered.

That part we'd all heard. The part we *hadn't* heard, the part Danny Gamage was telling, was about the Captain's bones searching for their proper resting place.

"So every Halloween, when the veil between this world and the next is thinnest, the grisly bones of Captain James rise up out of the waves at Pemaquid in search of his grave. His marble headstone stands in the old Pemaquid bone yard—*but he's not under it.* The stone is nothing more than a memorial, because they found no corpse to plant."

Danny Gamage knew he had a spellbound audience. "And every Halloween," he continued, "the poor Captain's bones clank up from the rocks at the lighthouse and clatter down the road to the bone yard, seeking their rightful rest at the empty grave."

"And how do people know?" gasped Mary Poole, a sixth-grader. "How do they know his bones are on the prowl?"

"They know," Danny said in a loud whisper, "from the trail of rotting, stinking seaweed leading from the road into the bone yard." We all held our breath. "It ends—" Danny said, pausing for effect, "*at his grave!*"

We gasped.

After a moment my brother Willy said, "Poor guy. It's like all he wants to do is be where he belongs. He wants to go—"

"—home," I finished.

"You're right," Danny Gamage said, and everybody agreed.

Brian Daggett said, "Too bad somebody can't be there to help the old captain into his resting place."

"What do you mean?" Willy asked.

"Well," Brian said. "Maybe if somebody *met him there* on Halloween, say, with a wooden crate, and *accepted his bones*—"

"Sort of like signing for a UPS package," Danny interrupted.

"Yeah," Brian continued. "Maybe if somebody accepted his bones, stopped them from roaming, the town fathers could bury the bones next day."

"Sure," Danny said. "On All Saints Day. It follows All Hallows Evening—Hallow E'en. It could be a sort of purifying thing."

"Making things right," Brian said. "After all these years."

"But who'd do it?" I chimed in. "Who'd meet the ghost at the cemetery?"

A deathly silence fell over the group, then all eyes turned on my brother.

"Aw, there's no ghost," Willy said, fidgeting.

"Okay," Danny Gamage said. "If there's no ghost, then there's no need to be *afraid.*"

That last word did it. *Afraid.* They had backed my brother into a corner, and before we knew it, the plan was set. On Halloween night we'd all go to the caretaker's shed at the old Pemaquid cemetery. Danny, Brian, Willy, and I would carry the wooden crate to the Captain's grave and wait for the ghost to arrive, then "invite" him to climb in. Once we had him, we'd call the others and haul the remains to the Town Office.

Danny, Brian, and the other kids figured Willy and me would keep mum about the bone yard caper, but we didn't. We mentioned it to Mr. Lombardi, the school's gym teacher. He was a handsome, muscular, black-haired man whom all the girls in school had crushes on.

He told us the Captain James shipwreck story was true, but that the searching bones story was the set-up for a Halloween prank, a trick played on some unsuspecting newcomers every couple of years. But he had an idea for turning the tables and asked us if we'd help him.

Halloween night was chilly, dark, damp. The air was clammy and made my flesh crawl. Ten of us met by the caretaker's shed.

"Ready, Brian?" Danny asked, getting a nod. "How about you two?" he then asked us, and we gave him the thumbs-up sign. "Wish us luck," Danny said to those staying behind, and the four of us headed off along the road toward the cemetery's front entrance.

Brian stopped short. "Hey, what's that?" he said, sounding alarmed. He pointed at the ground. Long strands of brown seaweed formed a trail at our feet.

"Uh-oh," Danny said. "It's him. The Captain. *Already here.*"

"You mean we're too late?" Brian said.

"I don't know," Danny answered.

"Let's catch up," Willy said, and Danny and Brian looked at him with surprise.

"You sure?" Danny asked, taunting. "You're not *afraid*?"

"Let's go," Willy said, leading the way. "We don't want to miss him."

Not far ahead we spotted the Captain's gravestone. Covering the grave site was a white sheet that practically glowed under the pale moonlight. It looked like a freshly made-up bed. We crept toward it cautiously.

"What's with the sheet?" my brother Willy asked.

"I haven't the foggiest idea," Danny Gamage said. "How about you, Brian? Any idea?"

"Nope," Brian said. "No idea whatsoever."

The two of them couldn't have sounded more phony.

We drew even closer to the grave. The sheet wasn't flat at all. It seemed to have the outline of a body under it.

"There's something under the sheet," Danny said.

"Or some *body*," Brian added.

The two of them set the wooden crate down.

"Maybe we should take a look under it," Danny said, his voice sounding very spooky.

In the darkness around us I could hear movement and catch glimpses of shadows shifting. One of the voices sounded like the tee-heeing of Mary Poole, who was supposed to be back at the caretaker's shed with the others. Our classmates seemed to be gathering around in anticipation of something.

"You grab one side of the sheet and I'll grab the other," Danny said to Brian. "Willy, you and your little brother open the lid of the crate. Maybe the old Captain is already under the sheet."

And that's the moment I'll remember—and regret—to my dying day. Danny and Brian yanked back that sheet from the grave, *expecting to see*—as they'd set up the prank every year—a skeleton; not the skeleton of Captain James, but the borrowed skeleton from the school science room, the skeleton intended to scare the dickens out of newcomers like me and Willy. Only what they saw wasn't a skeleton at all. What they saw was a huge, bloody-faced body covered in seaweed, lying there stiff as a board in yellow rain gear and a yellow Sou'wester foul-weather hat.

The color drained from Danny's and Brian's faces. And when the body began to spasm as if awaking, their eyes grew wide as saucers and their mouths dropped open in utter silence. The Captain's mouth opened and closed as he struggled to sit up, a croaking, cracking voice rising up from deep in his chest.

Danny and Brian screamed in honest terror, and

so did all the kids hiding in the shadows of grave-stones around us. Everyone fled the bone yard, screaming. Except Willy and I, who held our ground, expecting to enjoy a laugh with Mr. Lombardi in his yellow rain gear.

But the Captain shuddered and lay still. My blood froze and I felt chills creep over my skin. I looked at Willy, who shone his light at the grave.

"Mr. Lombardi?" he said. "Are you okay?"

A ball of pale light arose from the body and hovered above it a moment, then seemed to burst like a soap bubble, from which a pin prick of light floated skyward and disappeared far above us. Willy looked back at me and I could see the panic filling his eyes. We turned our attention back to the body lying before us.

"Mr. Lombardi," I said, my voice breaking. "You're scaring us." And for a moment I thought he might be part of the practical joke, too—not ours, but the other kids'—maybe doublecrossing us after we trusted him.

That's when the stench, the foul but sweet odor, hit our noses.

"Oh, God, that seaweed stinks," Willy said, shining his light on the body laid out before the headstone. Something like a mist—no, *steam*—seeped up from the arm and leg holes of the yellow slicker, and from under the cap.

Willy pushed me to take a step closer, but I couldn't. I was terrified. So he eased forward.

"Mr. Lombardi," he said, and when he shone the light where the gym teacher's face should have been, my brother winced, said "Agh," and began to retch.

I couldn't help myself then. I grabbed the light from Willy's hand and shone it where he had shone it. There was no face. Only a moving mix of worms and maggots.

"Oh my God," I gasped, wanting to retch, too.

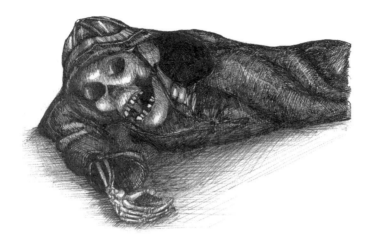

"Come on, Willy. We've got to get out of here." And we turned and ran for the road, then for town, babbling and crying all the way.

What the police found at the grave was a Sou'wester with a skull in it and a raincoat full of bones, really a skeleton covered with rotting seaweed. No worms or maggots, just bones picked clean of any flesh. The soil of the grave site had warmed up and softened, and the bones and slicker, and the skull and cap, had begun to sink in. Because they couldn't rule out foul play, they closed the grave off as a crime scene. But by the time the coroner arrived, the bones, skull, and yellow rain gear had sunk out of sight as if drawn down into quicksand.

The next day everything—bones, skull, raingear— was exhumed from the otherwise empty grave. This wasn't the skeleton from the school's science room, though. This one had a shock of thick black hair, and the clothing and identification belonged to Mr.

Lombardi. Dental records and x-rays later confirmed it was him. No one had an answer.

I don't understand how it could have happened, but even today I feel somehow responsible. Captain James, you're welcome. Mr. Lombardi, forgive us.

The Ice Fisherman

"The Ice Fisherman" isn't one for the horror magazines. It's a haunting atonement story nevertheless, and after first seeing daylight with two newspapers, *Peconic Bay Shopper* (September 1994) and *Green Mountain Trading Post* (March 1995), it appeared in such literary magazines as *Belletrist Review* (1995), *Potomac Review* (1995), *Reader's Break* (1996), *Potpourri* (1996), and *Vermont Voices III* (1999). It's also in the author's 1995 hardcover, *Unk's Fiddle, Stories to Warm the Heart.*

Cornelia watched from her parlor window, waiting for her brother Paul to appear on the frozen lake. He always walked onto the ice from behind the pines that made up the boundary between her land and his. They'd lived there all their lives—she, at seventy, occupying the family homestead she'd inherited thirty years earlier, and he, at sixty-eight, in his log cabin on the land their father had given him when Paul came back disabled from the war in Europe in 1945.

A dozen fishing shacks dotted the ice near the middle of the lake. Paul's was the light green one with the fluorescent orange door. Six or eight more fishing shacks—shanties, some folks called them—rested on the far shore on dry ground. Their owners either hadn't gotten them on the ice for the winter or had begun pulling them off early, anticipating an early thaw.

Paul's shack had been a more conservative color when he inherited it from their father, a dull brown, weathered with age. Except for the three years when her brother was away in the Navy and the year of his recuperation (not just from the physical recuperation but getting over the nightmares, one of which he claimed had begun recurring again recently after a forty year hiatus), Paul hadn't missed a winter of ice fishing on the lake since he was six. Fifty-eight years of fishing.

A snowmobile crossed the lake, coming first as a speck from the far shore where two dozen year-round camps had sprung up. There had been only two when Cornelia and Paul were growing up—one Uncle Freeman's, the other a rental cabin—and those used only in summer.

From behind the thermal-paned window Cornelia couldn't hear the whine of the snowmobile. Fine with her. She agreed with Paul that snowmobile racket shattered the peace of the place. Cross-country skiing was all right, but not noisy snowmobiling. Peace was what Paul loved more than anything, a sense of peace.

The snowmobile crossed the center point of the lake, weaving its way among ice fishing shacks as if negotiating an obstacle course. Once through the maze, it sped toward Cornelia's small dock. The driver was a boy—what, nine or ten—too young, she thought, to be riding the dangerous machine alone. She could hear their mother's voice railing against the evils of motorcycles in the 1930's, when Paul bought an old "hog" for the dirt roads between Lake Elmore and Montpelier.

"You be careful, Paul" Cornelia could hear her mother cautioning. "I want you home for supper in one piece."

The snowmobile slowed and veered before reaching the dock, then cruised parallel to the shore as if on drill parade. When the boy's hand went up in a wave, Cornelia's hand started up, too, in answer, but then she saw that Paul had emerged from the pines and was waving at the boy. A shadow crossed the ice between them—clouds overhead, no doubt—and Paul continued on toward his shack as the snowmobile kept following the shoreline and grew smaller.

Paul made his usual bee-line for the orange-doored shanty, pulling his ancient Flexible Flyer sled behind him. He limped in his usual way, first on his good leg with the insulated engineer's boot, then on the wooden one, mahogany from the knee down, saw-toothed heel plate on the end of the peg so it'd bite into the ice. He'd hobbled to his ice fishing shack thousands of times that way.

Cornelia smiled and shook her head as she thought once more of the irony. Paul's ship had been sunk in the North Atlantic by a German sub, and he'd had to adapt to a wooden leg. Yet here she sat day after day with two legs, each weak and unsteady, while her brother trekked onto the lake daily to fish.

Paul turned, looked Cornelia's way, waved. She returned it, their daily visual litany, a comfort. Only today's wave—what was there about it? Perhaps a heaviness, a tiredness she sensed rather than saw?

Her brother had never married. Cornelia had, but her husband Rudy has passed on fifteen years earlier. They'd never had children. Now it was just her and her brother.

Paul stood outside his shack, near where the white ice turned greenish-blue. A spring fed it from below, which was why Paul set his shack there year after year. Their father had said the Abenaki Indians believed the swirling spring was made up of spirits. Paul didn't know about that, he simply claimed the spring made it the best part of the lake for fishing.

"Springs are life-giving," he said. "Like circulating your blood."

She watched him disappear inside. It wasn't cold; in fact, the sun was bright and the lake's surface had been warming for days. Cornelia knew Paul wouldn't light the kerosene heater he kept inside the shack.

She knew her brother's routine, could picture him unfolding and setting up the blue canvas director's chair he kept on a nail. He'd use the rusty hatchet to break up any new ice that had formed over the hole in the night. Then he'd drop in his lines, settle back in the chair, and reach for the well-chewed cigar in the pewter ashtray on the shelf. He'd work the cigar around until it fit his lips and teeth with the snugness of a marble settling into a hole on a Chinese Checkers board. He never smoked the cigar, didn't even chew it. Just held it there in his mouth most of the morning and afternoon, removing it only to eat the sandwich and cookies in his lunchbox. When he left at mid-afternoon, he'd rest the cigar in its cradle on the lip of the pewter ashtray for next time.

"Don't hurt me if I don't smoke it," Paul would argue whenever she and Rudy had kidded him about the cigar. "Besides, unsmoked, a good cigar will last a week, maybe two."

Paul hadn't actually smoked a cigar since the day Kennedy died in Dallas, and he never said why he'd quit then. Unless he'd told Rudy, that is, Rudy who'd been not only his brother-in-law but his best friend. But if he had told Rudy, Rudy had taken the secret to his grave with him.

The sun cleared the peak to the east, and the thermometer outside Cornelia's parlor window read forty degrees. If it got much warmer and stayed that way, the ice above the springs would soften. It was already beginning to melt around the edges of the lake.

Cornelia felt a seed of worry. She'd seen it happen before, the melt above the spring. Shacks sank into the

ice as if in quicksand, tilting this way and that. Sometimes the lake would refreeze and the owners wouldn't be able to free them. Or if the shacks sank at final thaw of the season, they'd wait a month or two and retrieve them by boat, towing them home like dead whales.

Paul's had sunk only once, when he and Rudy had driven to Virginia for a Navy reunion. Things had warmed up unexpectedly. She could still remember how it chilled her to watch the coffin-shaped shanty sink gradually into the ice over those four days. In the end, only the roof was visible.

"I can always get another cigar," Paul had joked upon his return from Virginia, when he discovered the submerged shack.

Cornelia had wondered if it didn't remind him of the war and his ship's sinking, after which he and a group of his shipmates had spent two days adrift. Everyone but Paul had eventually slipped into the icy waters while awaiting rescue. Frostbite had claimed his leg and several fingers. He'd been decorated but insisted he didn't deserve to get the same medal the others got, which was why Cornelia kept the framed medal on her wall. Paul wouldn't allow it in his house. He spoke to no one about the sinking or his comrades' fate except Rudy, who confided to Cornelia that he thought Paul carried a load of unnecessary guilt.

The boy on the snowmobile zipped along the far shore, drove up the bank to a small frame house with smoke trailing from its chimney, and disappeared inside. Could he be done for the day? It was barely 9:30.

Another fisherman appeared three cabins east of the snowmobiler, wearing an insulated coverall outfit, fluorescent pink with black trim. If he hadn't walked toward a shanty, Cornelia would have thought him a jogger. He disappeared inside the shack farthest from

Paul's. The sun felt warm streaming through the window and made Cornelia sleepy.

The Regulator clock above the piano read one-thirty when she awoke. The sunlight that had put her to sleep had moved around to the other side of the house, and she felt cold. She moved to the kitchen for tea and a jelly sandwich, spreading butter on the bread before applying jelly, the way their mother had always done it. Paul had done it that way, too, until his heart problem, so now he skipped the butter.

"Hard to believe," he had said in honest disbelief. "A bum ticker. How can that be, with all the fish I eat?" Nevertheless, he had heeded his doctor, cut down on his fat, and lost weight. It was all he could do, since he wasn't a good candidate for bypass surgery.

Cornelia returned to the parlor window, sweater around her shoulders, lap blanket over her knees. Forty-eight degrees outside, and that from a thermometer reading in the shade. A gnawing returned to her stomach. She sipped her tea to calm it, and as she looked up from her tea cup—just for a second, the briefest moment—she was sure she saw Paul's friends standing together and looking at her, smiling, from a distance. She swallowed hard, almost choked, then she realized it was a reflection she was seeing in the window, a reflection of the World War II black-and-white photograph of Paul and his buddies that sat on the small table behind her. Except that Paul was in the photograph behind her. Had he been in the reflection she'd mistaken for the gathered group on the lake?

The jogging-suit fisherman stepped from his shanty and started the walk home. A string of small fish dangled from his hand. His free hand went up in a wave, and Cornelia saw that the snowmobiler had come back onto the lake and was waving. The boy showed a burst of speed the way young boys did in front of men, then headed straight across the lake toward her, bisecting it. From so far away, he resembled a teardrop dripping down her windowpane.

He turned the machine and put it into a skid before reaching Cornelia's shoreline, spitting up ice shavings as a figure skater did upon pulling up short. As he did, she felt the tiniest breath of air, chill air. A draft through a tightly shut window? It caressed her cheeks and a frisson of dread tingled along her spine. She drew her sweater tighter around her. Then the boy was flying across the ice again the way Cornelia had seen her father do sixty years earlier in his iceboat. This machine seemed less graceful, less fluid.

Paul stepped from his shack, stretched like someone awaking from a nap. He glanced toward Cornelia, then reached back in and pulled out a double string of fish, ten or a dozen. He held the strings up as if he were an Olympic athlete displaying a medal.

Cornelia smiled. So did Paul, and for the first time ever she caught a glimpse of sunshine reflecting off his gold-capped eye tooth. She was amazed to think she could see it at that distance. Was it because he hadn't smiled that broadly in awhile, or that the sun and the angle had never been right? It reminded her of an old movie she'd seen, where the hero's eyes and smile had flashed from the screen. Her brother, the hero.

That's when the snowmobile crashed through the ice. The boy went down, clutching the controls of the heavy machine. It never floated, not even for a moment, something it might have done had it been a four-wheeler with air in the tires. This was all metal and treads, and it simply disappeared down toward the bottom where the spring fed in. He must have let go the controls once he was underwater, and his snowmobile suit, perhaps because of the air trapped inside it, buoyed him to the surface. He thrashed his arms.

Cornelia could see his mouth opening and closing, but she heard nothing. Her eyes searched the far shore for the jogging-suit fisherman. He was gone, probably in his cabin.

She saw Paul hobbling fast toward the boy, booted foot on his good leg slipping, metal-toothed heel on the wooden peg gripping, biting the ice. Fifty yards to the boy, but Paul was closing the gap fast. The boy foundered and the snowmobile suit that had buoyed him now took on water, changing from life preserver to anchor.

The pink and black fisherman appeared in his doorway, perhaps to retrieve the fish from his porch. He glanced at the lake, dropped his fish, and broke into a run. He had two hundred yards to cover.

Paul was almost to the boy now, dragging his Flexible Flyer sled. He pulled up short of the ice break, swung the sled the way a mule-skinner side-arms a whip. The sled snapped toward the hole and splashed into the water in front of the boy's outstretched arms.

"Grab it!" Cornelia screamed. But the boy was too panicked and continued thrashing wildly. She pounded the window sill, yelled again, "The sled! Grab the sled!"

The man in pink and black looked like a runner now. A hundred yards to cover. Cornelia could see his mouth moving.

The boy flapped his arms twice more, looking the last time as if his hand might strike and grasp one of the runners of the sled. But the icy water turned his clothing to lead. He went under.

Paul let go the sled rope, planted his metal-tipped wooden leg as a pole vaulter plants the pole at take-off, and catapulted into the opening. Cornelia screamed as her brother vanished beneath the surface. The other fisherman reached the hole and stood staring blankly into it. Cornelia held her breath.

Suddenly the slushy water exploded as a head broke the surface. Two heads. In the midst of that upward-thrusting, breaching-whale motion Paul's strong arms heaved the boy out and onto the ice. The man in pink and black clutched the boy, then dragged him back from the hole. Paul rested his arms on the edge of the ice, and Cornelia saw him smile. The sun caught the gold-capped tooth again as he glanced her way. A second later she glimpsed the pain, the excruciating pain, as Paul's face contorted. His heart.

The other fisherman could do nothing.

Cornelia could do nothing. Then she saw Paul's hand come up—a salute perhaps—before his face relaxed and he slipped backward, backward into the icy water with his comrades, into the chilly sleep. She couldn't see him, but somehow she wasn't afraid either. She could picture him—drifting, drifting slowly downward, like a leaf in autumn, freed from the tree, drifting slowly downward into his comrades' open arms, drifting downward to rest, to rest in the life-giving spring.

Where Lions Hide

"Where Lions Hide" began as an environmental horror novel which used as its springboard an historical event, the 1941 appearance (but not sighting) of The Randolph Panther. The novel stalled, but a version of the first chapter appeared as a short story in *Green Mountain Trading Post* in January 1995. The environmental questions it raises are still disturbing. Why does *homo sapiens* kill other species? How do species adapt in the face of extinction?

Late in spring of 1941, six months before Pearl Harbor, the front-page news in U.S. newspapers was mostly about the war in Europe. Other news stories shrank in size and got swallowed up inside, deeper than page five. For example, a story about trappers in northern Maine reporting a quarter-mile wide fissure in the earth, which they estimated to be a mile deep, became a news tidbit, a curiosity. One story was a brief exception, however, about a Vermont mountain lion—*a catamount.*

Around dawn on Memorial Day 1941 a bloodcurdling scream split the silence above Thayer Brook in Braintree, Vermont. Farmer Fred Davis investigated in the daylight and discovered paw prints in his fresh harrowed field—eleven prints, to be exact, five and a half inches in diameter, five inches front to rear. The Randolph Fish and Game Club made plaster casts and said it was too big to be a lynx or bobcat. Whatever made the tracks had come down a nearby ravine, padded through the soft field, and vaulted over a four-foot, four-strand barbed wire fence.

The story hit the front pages of every major metropolitan newspaper in the Northeast. (The last set of catamount prints in Vermont, near the same area, was found in 1934 by a minister and Boy Scout troop from Chester on a camping trip. The Vermont State Museum authenticated them.)

By noontime the next day Braintree was swarming with people—reporters, outdoorsmen, naturalists. All the old stories and legends and tales about Vermont's Green Mountain catamounts—mountain lions, panthers, painters, pumas—were dusted off and retold. Even though Farmer Davis's farm was in Braintree, every news dispatch originated in larger nearby Randolph, so the cat came to be known in print as "The Randolph Panther."

Excitement ran high because Vermont's last authenticated mountain lion, the one hundred eighty-two pound "Barnard Panther," had been shot twenty miles south in Barnard on Thanksgiving Day 1881. A taxidermist stuffed the body for display at the state capital in Montpelier. No catamount sightings—no *verifiable* sightings, that is—had occurred since that Thanksgiving Day sixty years earlier.

But in the summer of 1941 sightings increased immediately. Several calves found slain near Riford Brook and Thayer Brook. A pony colt attacked and killed on Braintree Hill, its body dragged fifty feet from where it was killed, behavior typical of a big cat. The colt's forward shoulder and leg cleanly cut off.

Surveillance was set up in case the cat returned for the rest of its kill, but the wait was in vain. Either the cat was too smart or had moved on. Finally a $100 dead-or-alive bounty was posted and hunters covered the hills and valleys around Braintree and Randolph. But a dry summer made tracking difficult, and sightings dropped off except for one by a pair of brothers who claimed they shot at a cat farther north, around Moretown. Most hunters decided to wait for first snow and new tracks. The snowfall, however, didn't produce any tracks at all. And with the attack on Pearl Harbor in December and war raging in Europe, the headlines spoke more often of Panzers than panthers. The catamount story became yesterday's news.

Nevertheless, in Bethel, halfway between Braintree and Barnard, the 1941 and 1881 encounter sites, young Charlie Luce didn't forget about the Randolph Panther. Charlie figured the cat would head south, not north toward Canada as everyone predicted. Something told him it would go for Barnard—maybe because its ancestor had died there in 1881—the way dying elephants trekked to the secret burial ground. Charlie guessed its journey would take it along Fish Hill ridge from Randolph, past the Bethel granite quarry, down Christian Hill, and across the White River to Barnard. He couldn't have come closer with a crystal ball.

The Sunday after Easter 1942, Charlie and his beagle Topper hiked along the quarry railroad tracks up Christian Hill. As they'd done every morning for a month, they were bound for a deer yard north of the quarry, where they could wait in hiding. Charlie's hunting rifle hung by its sling from his shoulder. A shame he hadn't been able to enlist in the Army—after all, he was only twenty-eight—but a mill accident at sixteen left him with a metal hay hook where his left hand had been, so he was 4F. Even now, making his way over the hardpan of the quarry, he imagined himself going into battle. The ammunition belt around his waist made him feel invincible. The canvas knapsack on his back contained the bread and cheese his mother had packed for his lunch. Maybe he couldn't fight in the war, but if he could find and kill Vermont's only twentieth century catamount, he'd be somebody.

Charlie paused to look around the silent quarry. No work on Sunday, and what work there was had been slowed by the war effort. Most men Charlie's age had either enlisted or been drafted, leaving a handful of older men to work it. Only the day before it had been noisy with the clink and clunk of sledges and wedges splitting rock, the grunting of men and animals sledding the heavy blocks toward the railroad flatcars.

Topper veered toward a pile of rubble, nose to the ground. He was a fair tracker, though he often ended up cornering raccoons in the apple orchard or skunks under the porch. More than once Charlie'd had to rub the dog down with his mother's tomato sauce to get the skunk smell off. Topper sniffed intently.

Charlie scanned the rubble piles. *Probably just rabbit scent.* He thought he saw something move by a pile a hundred yards off. But in the bright sun and the white granite he could only squint, he couldn't focus. *Maybe a reflection.*

"C'mon, Topper," he whispered, changing course for the pile.

The dog didn't move.

"C'mon, Top, let's go." Charlie slapped the side of his thigh lightly a couple of times to get the dog's attention, and the beagle finally sidled up to him. He swung the rifle from his shoulder and cradled the barrel in the crook of his left arm, right index finger on the trigger guard.

The quarry went still. The birds stopped twittering. Even the breeze that had been rustling the buffer of hemlocks between the quarry and the woods ceased.

Charlie crouched and sneaked forward. Oddly, Topper stayed at his heel instead of leading.

A cloud passed over the sun, and the granite darkened. The air turned cold.

Topper froze. So did Charlie. Nothing moved by the rock pile, but they both sensed something was there. Twenty-five yards. Topper growled. *A scent? A movement?* The pile wasn't quite high enough to conceal a deer. Charlie inched left, circling for a better look. Topper approached directly, cautiously stalking. Charlie raised his rifle.

A noise to the left, in the brush. Charlie spun, swung his rifle around, feet seeking firm ground so he could squeeze off a shot if he had to. But his boot caught the brush and he pitched forward on his stomach. Something scuffled behind the rubble pile, something big, quick, startled, gone.

"Damn," Charlie muttered, sitting up. Topper stood beside him rather than pursue whatever it had been. He looked sympathetic as only beagles can, and Charlie patted the dog's head with his good hand.

"C'mon, Top, let's go see what it was." He got to his feet and the two of them walked behind the rubble pile.

"Holy geez!" Charlie gasped, stopping dead. He

had expected droppings, or tracks, or a rabbit carcass, but not what lay in front of him—the head of a black and white calf, a Holstein not more than a couple weeks old, eyes wide, no moisture coating them any more. The head had been sheared off at the shoulders, and the hide of its neck was caked with dried blood. Bits of flesh lay strewn nearby, but no bones and no carcass. Only the prey's head and neck had been carried to the quarry. Charlie noticed there wasn't any smell to it. The meat wasn't rotting. It hadn't been there long. The catamount's kill had been recent, probably during the night. Then a thought struck him—*It must have had enough or it wouldn't have left when we startled it, it would have stayed and fought for its kill.* He realized how close to trouble he'd just been, and was suddenly aware of the strong thumping of his heart in his chest.

The ground was too hard for tracks, but Charlie checked anyway. No droppings, either, but Charlie wasn't sure he'd recognize mountain lion scat if he found it. But one thing he did know—this was the handiwork of the Randolph Panther. His tripping over brush had startled it, and it had probably scrambled down the sidehill of discarded granite chunks into the ravine at the bottom.

An hour later Charlie climbed up into a makeshift hunting platform ten feet up a gnarled apple tree. He stuffed his jacket into the knapsack, sat down cross-legged in his observation post, and balanced the half loaf of bread on his left knee. In his right hand he gripped a hunk of cheese and hungrily tore off a mouthful. A few bits of cheese caught in the chin whiskers of his beard, and some fell onto the front of his shirt. The canteen Charlie's father had given him, the one he'd carried in the trenches in France in the Great War, hung by its strap from a stubby branch, a ready-made coathook. The rifle butt rested on the platform, the barrel leaning against the main trunk of the tree, front sight touching the canteen.

The apple tree provided a good vantage point; it was on the edge of a small clearing on the back side of a hill. Shoulders of granite outcroppings scarred the clearing, and Charlie had no doubt that eventually the granite quarry would sprawl and annex the deer yard. But for now it was a sanctuary, safe haven.

Moist fresh droppings showed the deer yard to be active. The week before, Charlie had stayed later than he'd planned, falling asleep in his perch. When he awoke, three pretty does stood in the center of the clearing. Charlie had kept silent then, watching for ten minutes until he had to leave before it got too dark to see the trail. The deer bolted when he climbed off the platform, but he was sure they wouldn't abandon the deer yard because of him. Now he found himself hoping the does would return, not for their beauty but because they might attract the catamount.

Charlie's mind drifted to the gray granite lion in front of the Bethel Library. He had sat astride it many times, wondering why the sculptor hadn't chiseled a Vermont catamount, but had instead opted for a thick-maned African lion. His mother said it had just appeared one day, along with a matching one in front of Randolph's public library six miles north. Although no one owned up to delivering or contributing the two gifts, rumor had it that it had been an immigrant stonecutter named Jerzey Talsky who worked at the Bethel quarry. He and his family had entered the country through New York City's Ellis Island, and when they began their journey to Vermont passed the New York Public Library, where Talsky saw a pair of the huge sphinx-like guardians—regal, full-maned stone African lions—watching over the entrance. Books and free libraries, people said Talsky declared (although he claimed he never said this) were America's visible symbols of freedom, as important as the Statue of Liberty, because they touched each individual's life. Most folks thought Talsky was the only stonecutter gifted enough to sculpt the lions, which they assumed he did in private. He would never admit to sculpting or setting up the Bethel and Randolph library lions, though, not even on his deathbed.

Charlie Luce had also wondered, while sitting astride Bethel's granite lion, what it would be like to stalk a lion, a panther, a tiger, or a catamount, and to shoot it like Jungle Jim or wrestle and stab it like Tarzan, to be the victor after a great battle.

Steadying himself by catching the hay hook hand around a branch, Charlie lifted a large hunk of the bread to his mouth, clamped his molars onto it like a vise, and pulled. It was tougher than a taffy pull, but finally a piece ripped free. *This is my body*, he could hear the old preacher at church saying, and the calf's head popped into his mind, *ripped apart for you*.

Charlie froze, the shred of bread sticking out the side of his mouth. Topper growled below, not moving a muscle. Without turning his head, Charlie scanned the clearing. Nothing moved. He breathed through his nostrils shallowly, listening, trying to pick up a sound, glimpse a movement, notice any change in lighting or shadows. With hardly any vegetation this time of year it would be almost impossible for anything to sneak around or through the deer yard unseen.

Topper growled again. Charlie's good hand, bulk of the loaf still in it, eased toward the rifle. A cloud passed in front of the sun, creating a fleeting shadow that crossed the clearing. But nothing else moved.

After an eternity, Charlie's fingers closed on the rifle and he began drawing it toward him. With both the loaf and the rifle in his grip, though, what was left of the bread threatened to slip free. *It'll make a noise and scare it.* He could feel the bread wiggling loose, but he couldn't do anything about it. He couldn't grip his rifle with the hay-hook hand alone. Out of the corner of his eye he caught a movement, a very slow movement, something long and sleek entering the clearing from the shadows under a huge pine.

The bread dropped, plopping into the leaves and brush behind Topper, startling him. The confused beagle leaped from his crouch to glare at the bread, the dog's sudden movement diverting Charlie's attention from the sleek shadow.

The beagle never had a chance. Just as his eyes turned from the bread to the shadow hurtling at him from the clearing, the cat was on him, sinking its teeth into the back of the smaller animal's neck and snapping it sideways the way barn cats execute mice after playing with them. But there was no playing with Topper. In a flash, with almost no bloodshed, no struggle, no howl, and hopefully no suffering, Charlie's companion lay dead on the ground.

Charlie's scream shattered the silence.

But the cat didn't run off. It lifted its burning eyes and stared up through the floorboard cracks at Charlie. Then it slinked away from the beagle's body and away from the tree in a gradually widening circle, straining to see clearer what had voiced the cry.

Full-scale terror threatened to seize Charlie, but he managed to pull at the rifle, good hand gripping the stock. The rifle's front sight tangled in the canteen strap looped over the branch. Charlie looked like a combination of Buddha sitting and Jesus on the cross—legs folded Indian-style, left hand extended and literally hooked on a branch, good hand directly opposite yanking on the tangled rifle. *I must look ridiculous.* It was all he could do to not laugh and cry and wet his pants all at the same time.

The cat screamed, and of necessity Charlie let go the rifle for an instant to unhook his left hand from the branch. He was quick, but couldn't recover fast enough, and the rifle swung by its front sights on the canteen strap, seemed to hang suspended in mid-air for an instant, then dropped off the edge of the platform, its butt striking Topper's rib cage with a thud.

The catamount sprang toward the platform and Charlie drew back involuntarily, sure he'd heard the wicked hiss of its claws slicing the air before it fell back to earth. Unable to think, Charlie retreated to the center of the platform and cowered there on his knees.

The cat began climbing the trunk. Charlie had no gun and could see that it was coming up fast. He pulled his fishing knife from its sheath. The blade was six inches, serrated on the back edge, razor sharp on the front. He gripped it tight, mind scrambling for an instant plan for how to best meet his attacker.

He'd barely risen to his knees when a paw appeared on the outside plank, bigger than he expected, the size of his own hand. A small grayish-brown pair of ears appeared, between them two cold blazing eyes. When it saw him eye to eye, the cat lifted its head and rolled it slightly as its scream filled the air. Charlie couldn't move. This was like nothing he'd ever seen, both beautiful and terrible.

It sprang. Charlie got his arms in front of his face and in the same movement ducked to the right, causing its front feet to pass over his left shoulder. But its chest caught him full there, the impact driving his left side back while spinning his right arm forward over the beast's back like a wrestler's half-nelson. He clutched the knife in his right hand but couldn't get the angle or leverage to drive it into the cat's ribs.

It recovered quickly and squirmed from its stomach onto its back, the opposite of a falling house cat righting itself in mid-air. Charlie found himself awkwardly astride his attacker, his weight on his left knee. Its claws slashed with lightning speed to lay open his cheek and shred his shirt and chest, the chest blow knocking Charlie to the edge of the platform on his back.

The cat flashed to its feet, sprang again. This time Charlie's feet went up defensively, catching it in the ribs in mid-spring and changing its direction. The cat's shoulder struck the branch with the canteen on it, and its left front leg caught for a split second in the canteen strap the way the rifle sight had gotten tangled earlier.

Charlie moved on it with his own animal-like speed, bringing his powerful left arm down like a blacksmith swinging a sledge to bury the hay-hook in the animal's bony breast. The cat's banshee scream split the air. It wriggled and rolled, its slashing claws shredding Charlie's forearm. Charlie screamed, too, a scream that welled up from some deep primeval pit he hadn't known existed within him. At that moment he wasn't different from the cat, wasn't separate. They were one, locked in primitive, mortal combat. All fear was gone.

Charlie raised the knife in his right hand, but the cat squirmed sideways, its movement carrying over the edge, but not far, for the cat's weight pulling downward only buried the hay hook deeper in its chest. Charlie lay on his stomach, peeking down, only his left arm hanging over. A sharp pain burned his left wrist as the cat, hung like a live steer on a slaughterhouse meathook, sank its teeth into his forearm. He screamed again, ears pounding, and struggled to his knees, lifting not only himself but the writhing catamount. On the ground below he caught sight of Topper's body and the rifle.

The cat bit down on his wrist again. He could see the blood on its teeth, his blood. With a last heave and a sound between a grunt and a scream he hoisted the beast halfway onto the platform the way a fisherman gaffs a shark and drags it over the gunwale. Before the cat could turn, he scissored his legs around it and squeezed with all his angry strength. It reached back and slashed his chin, cutting through to the bony part, barely missing cutting his throat.

But Charlie didn't miss. With the cat on his hook, his legs around its chest, the smell of blood in his nostrils, Charlie brought the razor-sharp fishing knife to his enemy's throat and drew it across hard, like a professional assassin. The cat screamed, then hissed as the air left its lungs, blood spraying from the wound into the air. Charlie held tight until the catamount twitched and went limp.

Charlie sat on the edge of the platform bleeding, exhausted, weeping. A latecomer might have mistaken the scene for a mourner cradling a dead friend. He sat that way until darkness fell, too weak to climb down, knowing that the life was ebbing out of him. *At least people will know I was brave, that Charlie Luce killed the last catamount.*

A light rain began to fall, then thunder crashed. A bolt of lightning lit the clearing, then another. There, in the center of the deer yard's clearing, he saw them— every time the lightning flashed—eight or ten of them. Not deer—*catamounts*, lined up, sitting on their haunches, front paws in a row like the pictures he'd seen of the Chartres gargoyles under the eaves. Waiting for him to die. Then they could claim whoever was on Charlie's lap, their brother, sister, parent, child. But then, in the last bright lightning flash before his vision faded, Charlie saw that one of them—no, two of them, next to one another on the end of the row, weren't cata-

mounts. They were much larger, had manes. Manes. Two African lions. Not gold, but gray.

Several items got lost in the war news over the next few months. There was a tidbit about the disappearance one night of two stone African lions—reputed to have been sculpted by immigrant stonecutter Jerzy Talsky—from in front of the Bethel and Randolph libraries. News, but hardly big news. The war was raging, and no one connected it to the other item.

A forest fire spotter in Maine reported seeing under pale moonlight a herd of animals slinking across a plain. Hundreds of animals—*mountain lions*, he swore—led by two large African lions. *Gray lions*. Gray, the entire herd following them—heads down as if tired, the spotter said, as if *sad* (though he wasn't sure how he sensed that, but he did)—following them north toward a huge fissure in the earth that trappers had reported the year before. The forest fire spotter's report was edited down, however, and became a brief paragraph—*a curiosity*—swallowed up by the war news the way Vermont's catamounts (and others) are swallowed up by the earth.

O R D E R   F O R M

Burt Creations

PLEASE SEND ME THE FOLLOWING:

QUAN.	ITEM	PRICE
_____	**A Christmas Dozen** Hard Cover Book ($17.95)	_____
_____	**A Christmas Dozen** Paperback Book ($14.95)	_____
_____	**A Christmas Dozen** Double cassette ($15.95)	_____
_____	**A Christmas Dozen** Double CD ($16.95)	_____
_____	**Unk's Fiddle** Paperback ($13.95)	_____
_____	**Odd Lot** Paperback Book ($14.95)	_____
_____	**Even Odder** Paperback Book ($14.95)	_____
_____	**Oddest Yet** Paperback Book ($14.95)	_____
_____	**Wicked Odd** Paperback Book ($14.95)	_____
_____	**Odd/Even/Oddest/Wicked** Four Pack ($54.80)	_____

Shipping & handling is $4.50 first item, $2.50 per additional item. Connecticut residents add 6% sales tax.

SALES TAX _____
SHIPPING _____
TOTAL _____

FREE SHIPPING ON ORDERS OF MORE THAN 10 UNITS

NAME _____

ADDRESS _____

CITY _____ STATE _____ ZIP _____

TELEPHONE _____ FAX _____ EMAIL _____

PAYMENT:

❑ Checks payable to: **Burt Creations**
     Mail to: 29 Arnold Place, Norwich, CT 06360

❑ VISA ❑ MasterCard

Cardnumber:_____
Name on card:_____
Exp. Date: _____(mo) _____(year)

■ **Toll free order phone** 1-866-MyDozen (866-693-6936 / Secure message machine) Give mailing/shipping address, telephone number, MC/Visa name & card number plus expiration date.
■ **Secure Fax orders:** 860-889-4068. Fill out this form & fax.
■ **On-line orders:** www.burtcreations.com
                        order@burtcreations.com

Burt Creations

PLEASE SEND ME THE FOLLOWING:

QUAN.	ITEM	PRICE
_____	**A Christmas Dozen** Hard Cover Book ($17.95)	_____
_____	**A Christmas Dozen** Paperback Book ($14.95)	_____
_____	**A Christmas Dozen** Double cassette ($15.95)	_____
_____	**A Christmas Dozen** Double CD ($16.95)	_____
_____	**Unk's Fiddle** Paperback ($13.95)	_____
_____	**Odd Lot** Paperback Book ($14.95)	_____
_____	**Even Odder** Paperback Book ($14.95)	_____
_____	**Oddest Yet** Paperback Book ($14.95)	_____
_____	**Wicked Odd** Paperback Book ($14.95)	_____
_____	**Odd/Even/Oddest/Wicked** Four Pack ($54.80)	_____

Shipping & handling is $4.50 first item, $2.50 per additional item. Connecticut residents add 6% sales tax.

SALES TAX	_____
SHIPPING	_____
TOTAL	_____

FREE SHIPPING ON ORDERS OF MORE THAN 10 UNITS

NAME

ADDRESS

CITY   STATE   ZIP

TELEPHONE   FAX   EMAIL

PAYMENT:

❑ Checks payable to: **Burt Creations**
Mail to: 29 Arnold Place, Norwich, CT 06360

❑ VISA ❑ MasterCard

Cardnumber:_____
Name on card:_____
Exp. Date: _____(mo) _____(year)

■ **Toll free order phone** 1-866-MyDozen (866-693-6936 / Secure message machine) Give mailing/shipping address, telephone number, MC/Visa name & card number plus expiration date.
■ **Secure Fax orders:** 860-889-4068. Fill out this form & fax.
■ **On-line orders:** www.burtcreations.com
                order@burtcreations.com

www.burtcreations.com

www.burtcreations.com

www.burtcreations.com